COVET

FORBIDDEN SERIES BOOK #2

DANI RENÉ

When everything seems dark, when you can't find your way, don't give up. There is always light and love at the end of the tunnel.

Life isn't an easy road, it's bumpy, it's riddled with potholes and cracks. Filled with ups and downs, but no matter how low the dips, remember, there's always ups. Within every bad situation, there will always be good to outweigh the fuckedupness of life.

Walk tall. Stand proud.
Be unique, but ALWAYS be YOU!

Hold your head up high, Kitten,
you don't want that crown to slip.

Covet
Verb [used with object]
To wish for, especially eagerly

THE DARK & THE LIGHT

In all darkness, there must be light.
In all life, there must be death.
In my heart, there must be you.
In your heart, there must be me.

PROLOGUE

Paige

JULY 2015

IT'S BEEN OVER A MONTH SINCE I WAS GIVEN TO HIM. ALMOST six weeks of my life has been spent in the dark. With the only light being him.

"This is what you were born to do," he murmurs with conviction, with emotion, with everything he thinks I need. Those are the same things I now covet. When I'm alone in my room. When he's out somewhere, doing God knows what, it's him I think about. It's our time here in this darkened room that reminds me my life isn't what I'd planned it to be. In this chilly space, where it's me and him, I'm reminded that I was stolen. We're not a couple. Only Master and slave.

There are things he does to me that make me feel. I've fallen down the rabbit hole and now I wish his actions meant more. He hides it so well. The emotion and affection. It's there beneath a cool exterior.

The mask he wears reminds me of a predator.

A wolf.

The color of a raven's feathers—black as night, with a splash of crimson which could be the blood he draws from the lashes on my body.

There's a deep-rooted anger in his dark eyes, but it's not aimed at me. Even though he enjoys taking it out on me, he never hurts me like I've heard the other trainers do to the girls.

Every time I meet his dark gaze, something human flickers behind it.

An outsider may think I'm crazy, and yes, I might be, but there's something caring about him. There have been many times in my training when he could have hurt me more than he has. But he's been... gentle. I suppose to most what I've been through is far from gentle. Does it make me a masochist to enjoy my caning? Does it make me crazy to enjoy when he makes me come after he's bound me and tortured my nipples and clit with clamps? Perhaps, but for my Wolfe, I'll do anything.

"Do you understand me?" *he growls in my ear, but I don't respond. Like an animal, a real living and breathing feral dog. He's in my cage, and given half the chance, I know he'll devour me.*

Before I was brought here, I never understood how women could want men to claim them. I didn't think there was anything sexy about it, but being claimed and owned by him makes me realize I want it. Suddenly, my leash is tugged, and I'm pulled to my feet.

"Look at me." *The order renders me speechless. I know I must obey, so I do.*

Our eyes lock in a searing gaze. There's nothing I can do but stare into dark orbs that remind me of cocoa. Such a conflicting range of feelings and emotions sweeps across the air between us like a tangible force—living and breathing between us.

"Do you know what you are?" *he hisses, even though I feel no anger in the words. Just confusion, pain, and a deep-rooted agony that's stifling.*

"Yes, Sir, I'm a slave." The words are ingrained inside me, deep in the core of my very being.

He leans in and my heart skitters. "Good girl," he murmurs, allowing his hot breath to fan over my ear. There's an innate need in his voice. Yes, men talk to me with desire and lust in their tone, but this... there's something different about him. The maelstrom of emotion that drips from his words hangs heavily in the air.

The first time he stalked into my room and laid his eyes on me, there was an innate connection between us. I noticed it, he did too, and our sessions took on a new set of rules.

As we spent our days together, I learned more about this predator. I've looked into his dark, anguish filled eyes and recognized the pain and guilt, but what stands out more than anything is the passion.

There was one poignant moment in our journey. When I knew he wanted more than we'd ever be allowed to have—the moment I bled, and he broke. Now I find myself at his mercy once more, waiting for the pain.

He rounds me, and the heat of his chest on my back has me melting into his body.

I can't see his face, but I can feel him. As if he's rooted within me. Even though what we have may be detrimental, lethal, there's no denying it. He is my tormentor, my savior, my lover. And I'm his forbidden fruit. I belong to Wolfe when no one is around. I am owned.

He tugs the leash and walks into the room where we have our training. A room that has seen so many tears, heard so many words thrown in anger and hatred. He pulls me onto a bench I've never seen before, dragging me from the memories.

He binds me to the black leather bench in silence. My feet are cuffed to either side and my hands are bound in front of me. Face down on the scented leather, I wait.

The silence always comes before the pain.

The calm before the storm.

That's what he's taught me.

"Close your eyes, little one." This is our routine. He tells me not to look when he's about to do something difficult. Harsh even. When I know blood will be spilled, he tells me to shut my "pretty green eyes." And I do. My God, I do. The agony I know will follow is going to leave me lacerated.

A gentle feathering against my skin startles me, then the thin, sheer material I was wearing is gone. Another feather light touch and then it starts. A whip cuts into me harshly. I've been spanked, paddled, and flogged, but this sends me into another dimension. The sound that catapults from me is inhuman.

Another bite into my skin and another.

Whack! Whack!

Liquid oozes down my back. I can feel it trickling down like syrup drizzled over sweet treats. Nothing could ever prepare a person for something like this.

The agony. The pain. The torment.

But I don't beg for reprieve, I take it like he taught me. All I feel are the silent, salty emotions racing down my cheeks. Every time he does this—that we do this—it's different. The mood shifts, the emotions choke me. I want this, but only because it's him. I need this, because he's the one delivering the blows. And as my tears fall, they drip like a poison. But they won't kill me, as much as I wish they would, I'm still *here. I'm still falling for a man who hurts me. And with every lash, with every sting, he soothes me where I need it most. He appeases my soul.*

"Good girl. I'm proud of you," he murmurs, soft lips on mine. Those words. They seep into the wounds now scorching my back. He unlatches me, and I'm freed from my confines. Every move I make feels as if my skin is on fire. This isn't pain, this is so much more, so much worse. And as I meet my tormentor's stare, I realize this has hurt him as much as it did me. He doesn't realize how much his eyes tell me. How much they convey all the emotion he stores behind the mask. It's clear as day. Love.

I want to tell him to steal me away. I want to say so much in that moment, but I don't. We just stare each other down for a long while.

"You did well today, little one." His soothing tone eases the ache on my back. "Stay down, I need to see to these so they don't scar." He pushes me down roughly, and I obey. The cold balm he rubs into my wounds stings, but it also adds a sense of serenity. "Time to get some sleep, pet. You'll be busy tomorrow," he says and I can hear the pain in his words. Even though they calm me in their own way, there's one confession I want from him which never comes.

I want to ask more questions, but I know I'll never get my answers because that's not what he can offer me.

ONE

Paige

TODAY IS SUPPOSED TO BE FUN, EXCITING EVEN. IT'S ANYTHING but. I've taken my time this evening. Preparing for something that I've been dreading most of my life. I'm now an adult. Ready to take on the world. Once tonight is over, I'll be the person who my parents have taught, cared for in their own cold way, and nurtured to become the woman who's meant to rule. To run what they believe to be an empire.

My parents have been planning this day from the moment I was born. The day my mother went into painful labor—which she loves to remind me about—is the day my fate was sealed in a neat little package. Paige Madden, daughter and heiress to more money than I can even think about.

Growing up in this world where I've had to put up with bodyguards and people following me around has become second nature. Every breath has been counted, each step has been guarded. I'm the pristine princess. And today I'm meant to be celebrating freedom. I'm eighteen, and my father has agreed to allow me to leave home. I've received my acceptance letter to college and I can't wait to drive out of those tall, raven-colored gates with the gold trim and not look back.

"Paige, why aren't you dressed?" I turn to find my mother dressed in a long, flowing scarlet dress. The sleeves hug her slim arms, and when she walks, it's as if a million little stars twinkle in the material. But there's nothing ethereal about her. When families have money like we do, there are always secrets. And the Madden household runs rife with them. Those that lurk in the murky corners. That can break apart a family, and bring down the name they hold so dear.

I glance down, taking in the mask she's holding, which matches the red of her dress. Her long auburn hair is twisted into a tight bun on the back of her head. Severe. That's how I'd describe her if anyone ever asked. Only, they're too scared to ask, because if they did, they'd be shunned by the elite society we live amongst.

It's obvious from looking at me that I'm my mother's daughter—she's an elegant, poised red-head and so am I—but that's where the similarities end. "I'm just finishing up my make-up. I'll be ready in a few minutes." She huffs, tugging at the material of her dress that hugs her slim frame. My mother's always been a waif. Since I can remember, she's been one of those women who'd hide on a day when her hair wasn't pinned in place. Never leaving the house if she didn't have make-up on.

She's hovering. There must be something on her mind because my mother doesn't normally hover. Her cold demeanor is something I've become accustomed to. "What is it mother?" I question as I turn to regard her in the reflection of the mirror.

"Your father's partner and his son will be coming tonight. Daddy would like to make a good impression. I'd like you to keep his eldest son entertained." With an imploring gaze, her eyes meet mine, the same jade hue as my own.

I've always been expected to portray an air of elegance and maturity far beyond my eighteen years. In everyday life, and by attending parties that were better fit for adults rather than a child. Stuffy suits and expensive gowns. Sometimes I think I've had to grow up too fast. My childhood was filled with talk about mergers and acquisitions. About political climates and corporate contracts.

This however, will be the first time I'll see the man my father has told me about. He decided to partner with Harlan by investing millions in a business that I've overheard him whispering about in his office. Something deep in my gut tells me that it's not legal in the least bit.

Since I turned sixteen, Daddy has educated me, making sure I understood contracts and legal jargon that to me, meant nothing. It's not where my passion lies. I've never wanted to be in the corporate world that is filled with rules and regulations.

Tonight, they've invited this man, along with his infamous eldest son to my birthday party. My mother hasn't stopped rambling about how handsome his son is and how she'd like to see me with him. I, however, would like to make my own decisions when it comes to who is going to one day take the one precious thing I have held on to, my virginity.

"Yes, Mother. I will be as gracious as I can," I retort with a bite in my tone, which has her nodding tersely. We normally get along, but when she forces me to do something, we tend to butt heads.

"I just want to make sure we leave a good impression on Mr. Wolfe. He's a well-regarded man. It would be good for your father's reelection for senator which is coming up and Harlan can help with the focus on your Dad." My father is running for senator a third time in a row. So far, he's served twelve years in office. I'm not sure why they're so concerned though. Since he's been partners with Harlan, there has only been one opposing delegate for my father.

He's always been more of a businessman than a doting dad. I love him dearly, but deep down, I wish he'd show me the kind of love I've seen dad's on TV offer their daughters. I suppose, being from a family like ours, I had to get used to having an absent father. All the girls at the private school I attend have the same problem I do. Work is always more important than family.

I don't respond, merely nod at her request. "Thank you," she says in her rigid tone, then pivots on her sparkly, silver heels and leaves me to get dressed. My mother expects me to entertain a man I have no inkling to talk to.

Taking in my appearance, I notice how the black corset I chose tonight hugs my curves. It's beautiful, shiny and delicate. Slipping the black chiffon, floor-length dress from the hanger, I pull it on and as it cascades down my body, the sheer material feels heavenly against my smooth skin. It's the color of night with a thin silver belt that wraps around under my breasts. I've opted for short sleeves because in this heat, I'll never survive stifling clothes.

The heels I've chosen are a delicate silver sandal with just enough height to put me at a comfortable five foot eight. My waist-length red hair falls down my back in loose waves, and the mask I'm wearing is jet black with red gems placed intricately between my eyes and over each brow. It's in the shape of a bird born of fire, the Phoenix.

Taking one last long look in the mirror, I head to the door and leave my bedroom. The door clicks closed behind me with an ominous sound. Something stirs deep in my gut, call it intuition, but I realize that something is going to change tonight. Something that's going to alter the course of my life. I just don't know what.

The living room is opulent. Dim lighting from the chandelier and candles give it an ethereal feel. Although, the room isn't filled with angels tonight, it's packed tight with devils. My father's business associates haven't always been above board, and I know more than he thinks I do.

Yes, I may only be eighteen, but I've grown up around this life, around the secrets that are hidden behind closed doors. I've overheard his meetings, phone calls. The small grate in my bedroom affords me a front row seat to conversations I'm sure he'd rather I not hear. When I'm away at school, I'm sure I miss a lot more. And that's how I've still not come to meet Harlan Wolfe yet.

"Paige, come here, pumpkin." My father's deep rumble comes from behind me. It's enough to give me shivers. As I near him, I notice the older man beside my father. His salt-and-pepper hair is thick and shiny. The mask that hides his face resembles a hawk—black with a silver streak of lightning across one eye. "This is my partner, Harlan, and his son, Samael." I drag my gaze up to cobalt eyes that pierce me, as if they're looking straight into my soul.

I can't see his face because of the charcoal mask that covers it, but I can see his mouth curl into a smirk that's dark and devilish.

"A pleasure." His voice is smooth like silk, but holds an edge to it. The tone has my stomach tumbling unwillingly with a flurry of butterflies.

"I'm sure the pleasure is mine," I murmur as he lifts my hand to his lips. They're soft and warm, causing a jolt of heat to race through every bone in my body, leaving me breathless.

"It will be," he promises illicitly. "Care to dance?" I nod. Leaving our fathers in the wake of the strange yearning swirling between us, I step beside him until we reach the open area reserved for dancing. A slow tune starts, and I recognize Aaron Richards singing "My Hell," and I wonder if it's as ominous as I think. We weave around the floor. He leads, I follow. "There's something intriguing about you, Red." He gazes down at me curiously. A scorching gaze simmers below his mask.

His hand drops to my lower back as he pulls me along with him. Our bodies move in a fluid motion. "There is?" I question, cocking my head to the side as I regard him.

"Yes." The one-word answer leaves us in silence for the rest of the dance, and as it comes to an end, he releases his hold on me and offers a curt bow.

"Thank you," I murmur, responding with a curtsey. Everything in my life is formal with nothing out of place, and the respect I was taught to show others is blindingly clear as I turn to walk away.

The night goes on with many more introductions, and by the

time I glance at the clock, it's almost midnight. A moment alone allows me to take in the remaining guests. The party is still in full swing, everyone chattering about money, deals, and contracts, all the while drinking expensive champagne and eating the canapés my mother ordered.

Taking the opportunity to make my escape, I head out to the garden.

Our property is enormous, and the pristine grounds are immaculate. Stepping into the night, I take a calming breath. It's quiet outside since everyone is more interested in what's happening inside. "Should you be out here alone?" The thick, decadent tone of Samael startles me, and I spin, tripping on the step, but before I hit the ground his strong arms wrap around me.

His broad chest is flush with my breasts, causing my nipples to harden against the material of my corset. I might be a virgin, but I'm no stranger to lust and desire. "Thank you," I breathe as he straightens me. Instead of releasing me from his grasp, he tugs me against him as if we're dancing to the music that filters from the ballroom. His mouth is close to mine, but he can't kiss me because of his mask. In that moment, I'm cursing the fact that we had to have a masquerade ball.

"I shouldn't do this, but no one can stop me," he growls, and the predator staring at me looks as if he's about to devour me. He reaches up with one hand and pulls off his mask, giving me the full effect of Samael.

Tanned, masculine jaw with a light dusting of stubble. His straight pointed nose is elegant, almost classic. Those cobalt eyes—now matching the midnight sky—stare with hunger under thick eyebrows. Dark and brooding, he drinks me in. His full lips have me wetting my own. The butterflies from earlier awaken in my belly reminding me what it's like to be this close to a man. My ex-boyfriend wasn't anything like Samael, but I used to feel the excited tingle race through me in the beginning of our relationship.

My gaze drops to his lips, I want to taste them, to taste him.

Before I can ask what he wants to do, his mouth crashes down on mine. The longing tightens everything south of my belly button, attacking me with vengeance, just like this man is devouring me. His tongue licks my lips, each one fevered as he sucks them into his hot mouth. His pearl-white teeth graze them, biting down causing a soft whimper to fall from me each time.

A low growl rumbles through him, animalistic, feral, and powerful. Everything about him is dominating. As his hand grips the hair at my nape, positioning my face just right for him to lash me with his tongue, I open, allowing him into my body. He may not be taking my virginity, but he's fucking me with everything he has.

Our tongues dart around each other, dancing, teasing, taunting. He presses me against the enormous cement pillar. His erection pushing into my thigh as he steals my breath along with my moans and whimpers.

My hands reach up, but before I can touch him, he grips both my wrists. Holding them at my sides, pressing them against the cold concrete. Without warning, I feel his teeth—razor sharp—bite down on my lower lip, while sucking it hard into his mouth. I feel the skin break. He laps at the crimson liquid that seeps from the cut and as much as it should have scared me, it doesn't and my body is on fire for him.

Quickly, he steps back and releases me. Leaving me a frenzied mess, he spins on his heel, puts his mask back on, and saunters away.

I hear the words fall from his lips just before he's out of earshot.

"Soon, Firebird."

TWO

Kael

As I head into my bedroom with a towel wrapped around my waist, I can't help thinking about the new girl I'm going to be training today. I've heard her name before, I've seen her from a distance, but never had the chance to talk to her.

As I get the usual clothes I wear when with my pets, my mind plays back on the day my life changed. I wasn't ready. I fought against it from the moment I knew what fate had in store for me. The only person I trusted was my best friend. The memory plays in my mind like it happened yesterday.

"Fuck!" Axel stares at me. He's the only one who knows what I've been told to do. "I'm fucking twenty years old. He wants me to start now?" I glare at my best friend, but there's nothing he can do to fix this. My father is a tough man, and if I refuse, I'll be in a world of pain. That's the only thing my father knows how to do—how to inflict pain. Whether it's on his sons or his daughter, or any of the whores he allows into his bed.

"Kael, man, you need to go. I'll see you later," he informs me. I

push up from the chair and grab my jacket. He's right. When I get summoned by the devil himself, I need to make sure I'm there as soon as fucking possible. I was late for a meeting once and he made sure I felt it for days after.

"If you head to the party, let me know. I may need to sink into some pretty girl to get the filth of what I'm about to do off my body." My frustration is evident in my retort. Heading down the hallway, I hear my best friend's response.

"You just want pussy. Don't make excuses." Axe smirks and nods.

He knows what my father does. What the Wolfe family business is. My Maserati sits waiting for me as I near the parking lot of the bar I just left. A sleek platinum beauty. But before I can escape, I hear my name. "Kael Wolfe, isn't this a surprise?" I turn to find the familiar bleach blonde, blue-eyed woman staring at me. I can't remember her name, but I sure as hell remember how she swallowed my dick.

"What do you want?" I pin her with a glare, but she doesn't even notice. This is my problem. I hate when they cling. Pushing the remote to unlock the car, I pull open the driver's door, leaning on the frame. Her gaze falters for a second, but she swiftly straightens her posture, offering a smile.

"You didn't call," she murmurs. Her attempt at being seductive fails because I see through the tension in her shoulders. Shrugging, I smirk at the insecurity that laces her tone.

"I don't hit it twice, sugar. I have to go." With a cocky wink, I slip into the plush leather seat. Once the door is shut, I push the Start button and the engine purrs to life. I fucking love this car.

Before I head onto the main road, I notice she's still standing there. The pout on her Botox lips causes me to shudder. I must have been wasted when I thought she was beautiful.

I've gotten used to my life as it is, no relationships. I'm not allowed to have any commitments because when it comes to my father and his business, there are strict guidelines to follow. No long-term women hanging around. No love. There's no room for that in my life. His rules are law. I can't disobey because the path I'm about to follow will lead me straight to hell.

If I wasn't born into this family, I'd have chosen one without the dark shit that is our legacy. As much as I'd love to walk away, I can't. The blood that runs through my veins is Wolfe blood—toxic, poisonous—and as it slowly siphons the goodness from my heart, it blackens my soul.

Pulling up to the estate, I wait for the large, ornate metal gates to slide open. The security at the Wolfe compound resembles a prison, just short of giving blood allows you entrance. As the foreboding house comes into view, I inch closer to the nightmare that is Wolfe Enterprises headquarters. My father runs his devilish shit from home. The grounds house the mansion, which is split in two sections: our living quarters, and the East Wing where the girls live. The club is in the same section, and that's where they're trained. My older brother, Sam, has taken to this business easily, and I'm afraid he's going to turn into my father. The change in him has been immediate. His nickname, The Grim Reaper, is not to be taken lightly.

Once I pull into my private garage, I get out and head inside. The kitchen's always been my favorite place in the house, and as I stroll through it now, the scent of dinner wafts through the air.

"Kael, how are you?" Our chef is a short stout woman in her fifties, and the smile she offers is motherly. Sometimes I wonder what she's doing in the wolf's den, but she seems happy enough turning a blind eye to the number of girls who come and go. When my mother died, she looked after the three of us, caring for us in a way that made us feel as if we had the love of a parent, since my father was too interested in his business to care about three kids.

"I'm good, Hesta. It's been a long day, and Dad has summoned me." By the look in her eyes, she knows what this means. She's been through it with my brother, and now me.

"Good luck, Kael," she murmurs as I head out of the kitchen and through the house. It's empty, and I wonder where everyone could be. The ground floor is silent, where normally there'd be masses of staff rushing around, preparing for tonight. The sweeping staircase looms before me, and as much as I'd like to rush upstairs and hide out in my wing, I can't, so I head in the opposite direction. To the basement.

Most may picture a dark dungeon, but the club is far from it. Decked in rich auburn and dark chocolate colors, the place looks like an elite gentleman's club. My father's office door is open when I reach it. Before I push it open, I hear him talking. "Yes, we'll collect her tomorrow. I'm about to talk to Kael."

Suddenly an ear-piercing scream echoes through the hallway, and I realize my brother must be playing with one of the toys. My brother likes blood. He loves to see the deep crimson seeping over smooth, creamy flesh.

"Come in, Kael. Don't skulk in the shadows." My father's deep, booming voice filters through my thoughts, and I head into the Wolfe's den.

I shake my head trying to clear my mind of the memory.

As much as I try, I can never forget the day I became someone I despise. It was the day my father took me into Caged and showed me what he wanted from me. *We're here to train girls to take punishments.* The club is well known for its clients enjoying BDSM. The only thing we're not allowed to do is fuck the girls, or get personal. The men who frequent the club pay a high price for the pleasure of taking a virgin.

"Brother, I had a taste of your new pet last night." Sam's gravely tone crawls over my skin. It's been six years since I was brought into Caged and told about what lies in my future. My father insisted I become part of the underground world our family started generations ago. As much as I should be used to it, I'm not. My brother however, he's different. Where I'm less violent, he enjoys the blood and he taunts me every time I get a new girl. He's never kissed any of them. I wonder what makes this one so different.

I was told she'll arrive today, and I'm getting ready to meet her in an hour. Apparently, she's a feisty redhead. When my gaze lands on him, I can tell he drew blood. As if he's a fucking vampire or something.

"And? Is she sweet?" I'll play his game if he leaves me to do my job. I'm not stupid. I've been doing this for long enough to know that she's nothing more than a toy. Something to be broken in. Like a dog when first brought home. I wonder if this puppy bites.

"Fucking delectable. The little firebird made me so hard, I

almost took her right there in her garden. I bet she's still a virgin from the way she moaned as I sucked on her tongue." He smirks, leaning against the doorjamb of my suite and looking overly confident as usual. "Dad was going to gift her to me, but decided otherwise. Also, since you couldn't be bothered to attend the gala last night, I figured I'd see what the fuss was about with this one."

"Great, I'm glad you had your fun. Now it's my turn." I pull on my black hoodie, covering the mask I wear when I enter the girls' rooms. Before I'm out of earshot, he utters the words I dread.

"Make her bleed, brother, because if you don't, I will."

Dressed in an impeccable suit, his blue eyes chill me and his words slice through me like a sharp blade because I still wish he wouldn't become the savage he so clearly is. I always wanted my older brother to be someone I could look up to, but I can safely say I've lost him to this darkness. Without responding, I head out and leave the venomous snake behind. There's no love lost between him and me. I used to think he was my hero.

When the realization hit and I saw the sadistic bastard that lies behind the smile, behind the lies he likes to portray, I knew there was no longer anything good inside him. The darkness of our bloodline has taken over, and he's no longer a man, but an animal.

The hallways are quiet as I stride toward the room where I know she's waiting. Perhaps patiently, maybe not. The girls will be at work now, so the new pet and I will have the floor to ourselves. Sam said she's in the room at the end of the hallway, and as I near the bedroom, a soft scent of lemongrass hits me. Reaching for the handle, I push the door, swinging it wide. With a quick glance inside, I find her sitting against the headboard, her legs hugged against her chest and her head on her knees. Fiery red hair hangs like a curtain, shielding her from me.

This room is my favorite. Deep reds, with a touch of silver and black that accentuate the plush furnishings. It's exquisite, everything a princess could want. Even after six years of walking into one of these rooms, I still get this sinking feeling. All I want to do is escape. But then I remind myself that won't be happening.

The girl lifts her head when she hears my footfalls, her deep green glare enough to make me smile. I take her in once I close the distance between us and recognize the face I've dreamt of for a year now.

Paige Madden.

Her father's a partner in Wolfe Enterprises. I'm momentarily shocked at how beautiful she is up close, then distracted when she lowers her legs and the blanket she had around her falls open. She's beautiful. Dressed in a skintight pastel pink top, which hugs a pair of incredible tits. Her fiery red hair is a mass of waves, framing a delicate yet fierce expression.

"Hello, little one." My voice is a deep rumble, which sends a slight shudder through her which I notice immediately.

Sitting up, she narrows her eyes, shooting daggers at my

masked face. "Who are you?" She juts out her chin, regarding me with rage dancing in those orbs that remind me of the finest emeralds.

One word comes to mind when I look at her.

Exquisite.

I've never officially met her, but I've known of her, seen her from afar. I knew she'd be brought here one day, but the reason why she's here is what has the guilt threatening to choke me. Not because of what I'm about to do to her, but because her own father is allowing it to happen. I step through the doorway and her sweet perfume invades my senses, taunting me. No wonder my brother was so enamored by her.

"I'm your trainer." My tone is calm as I near her, but my response earns me a huff. It's adorable. Her feistiness will need to be snuffed out. She can fight me all she wants. Her strength makes me wonder how long it's going to take me to climb inside her mind and undo her from the inside out. Her fire burns now, she thinks she won't break, but she will. I know she'll bend to my will soon enough, and I'm going to make sure her obedience is rewarded—like the pet she's meant to be. "On your knees." The order earns me a glare, and I chuckle. There's no humor in it, though. I fix her with a rigid glare, and it's then that she realizes I'm not joking. "I said, on your knees. If I must keep repeating myself, we're going to have a problem, pet, and you're not going to like it." My tone is one of pure dominance. Dripping with hunger to see her body tremble.

"Why do you call me that?" she questions. Her defiance is adorable. It makes me want her, like my brother does.

"Because that's what you are. What would you prefer I call you?" I question, but it immediately comes to me when she shifts and the light catches the slight golden strands in the bright red of her hair. "Firebird?" The word immediately has her staring at me in shock.

"Samael?" The way she breathes my brother's name has jealousy coursing through me.

"No."

"My father—"

"Your father can't do shit for you now. Get on your fucking knees. I'm not asking again." Fear licks over her features while her red hair spills down her back. She's ethereal, innocent, and decadent. So beautiful. It's like a drug to me, and I'm certain this woman could become an addiction. In this moment, staring at a woman who's as fiery as she is beautiful makes me want to take her. To have the control over a lithe body and inquisitive mind.

"But why am I here? This isn't—"

Leaning in with my face close to hers, I inhale her sweet scent. "When I tell you to be quiet, I mean it. I may seem like a nice person, but I'm not. Stop asking fucking questions that you do not want the answers to," I hiss in her face, and as much as I want her to play the submissive and stay silent, I can see the fire dancing in her emerald eyes. This fiery girl comes across as a fighter. She's different. She won't be easy to break, but she will shatter. They all do.

As she drops to her knees, I feel lust course through my veins, heating my blood. My body is an inferno of need. Her perfection seems to overflow from her exquisite form. The supple porcelain skin that is mine to mark as I wish has me licking my lips.

I want her. More than I've wanted any other toy.

Her eyes meet mine, strength oozes from her pores like a perfume, and I can't help but inhale and savor the scent.

"Good girl," I whisper and goosebumps dot her flesh. Two words that can have any woman submitting. Crouching in front of her, I meet those deep green pools. Our faces are close. Her breath quickens along with her heartbeat. The pulse in her neck is erratic as she watches me. I lift the collar I'm holding and close it around her neck. The small locket is an intricate jewel in the shape of a wolf's head.

Our family crest.

"I'm not a dog. Don't treat me like one," she hisses with anger marring her beautiful face. As I take her in, I see how incredibly intoxicating she is.

Reaching for her face, I stroke her cheek with the pad of my thumb, reveling in the way she shudders. I know it's more from fear than desire, but the act alone makes me want to see her unravel under my touch. Her skin is smooth, silky to the touch.

No blemishes, no make-up, all natural perfection.

"You're a pet. You'll be trained by me. If you're good, I will ensure you're not hurt. And, trust me, the other trainers aren't as nice as I am. So I need you to trust me. Okay?" I don't know why I'm warning her. It's not something I've ever done with any of the other girls.

She doesn't answer, merely nods.

Don't get personal.

My father's words haunt me. I rise, tugging the leash, and she pushes to stand. "Kneel." Her eyes lift quickly, regarding me in confusion. "You're a pet. You crawl."

Realization clouds her features, and I wait for her to fight me. Her mouth opens, but she doesn't say anything. Her head drops and she moves on all fours. It's the hottest thing I've ever fucking seen.

I lead her to the room where I take all my girls, filled with toys of the trade. Most of the girls enjoy it in here. Those are the masochists. They enjoy the pain I bestow on their bodies. I wonder how much pain my little firebird can take.

The slow walk down the hallway is silent, but I can feel the tension radiating from her. Shoving the door open, I pull her inside and shut it behind me. The dim light doesn't allow her to see what's hidden in the shadows, and it's a good thing, because if she could, she'd be running in the opposite direction. "I want to you stand. Raise your arms." She obeys, and my cock thickens at her submission. I want to look into her eyes, to meet the questioning gaze, but I don't. Even I can't see them. Anger and fear ring off her like a melody summoning me to hell. I'll be there soon enough.

The wall beside us has rope of every color adorning it. I grab the crimson one that's thin, silk, and soft to the touch. With care, I bind her wrists and she hisses in...frustration? Anger?

Once she's conditioned to being bound, it will become second nature.

"Can you tell me your name?"

Her question halts me. Confusion clouds my judgment, and I almost tell her.

No other toy has ever asked me my name. They've never had the courage to.

"No," I bite out. I may sound like an asshole, but I can't have her growing attached. She'll soon be working, and my time with her will be over. It's easier that way.

"I'm Paige," she says, but I don't stop. I grab a blade and slice through the thin material of her top. As it falls from her slim body, I can't help my cock growing painfully hard. Her white bra is cupping perky tits that are just about a handful. My mouth waters, and I know I'm going to have to get a taste of them. "I'm eighteen," she continues, but once again, I ignore her.

Gripping the leash, I lead her over to the bench and sit her down. There's no time to play nice. I need to get her trained and ready so I can walk away. My heart lurches in my chest as unbidden anger roils through me. I don't want this girl to be in this world. She sits with her hands in her lap, her head bowed, and her legs pressing tightly together.

The perfect submissive.

Don't get personal.

THREE

Paige

"Paige." He turns to me meeting my stare head on, I can tell he's at war with himself by the sadness that seems to glisten in his eyes. There's guilt there too, it's clear as day as he gazes at me for a moment too long. Something inside niggles at me as my fear and curiosity meld together. It's like staring directly into the eye of a storm—dark, frightening, yet intriguing—and I shudder at the thought.

Fear stills me for a moment, and I find myself rigid. Rooted to the spot. Watching him, I wait for his next move, but when he doesn't shift, I decide to speak.

"I want to know why I'm here," I say with a fake confidence that I don't feel. "Please?" My question is low as I drop my voice to a whisper. His gaze is heated when he pins me with it. "I just need you to talk to me. Please?" From the way his body tenses, the way his dark eyes flit around the room I can tell he's trying to ignore me. The silence is too thick, filled with tension as he works with the straps of leather. As I watch him, I see more than he thinks and recognize the anguish in his quick glances.

I should be afraid, but I'm confused as well. They both war inside my head. Screaming at me to figure out what's going on, but also to behave so they don't hurt me. Suddenly, he stops, stares directly through me and spits the words as if they taste like venom on his tongue. "You're here because you fit the description of the product we provide. Men want sweet, innocent girls."

His words shock me into silence. My brain falters, trying to make sense of what he just said. Red-hot fear races down my spine and my body quakes with horror as the words start making sense. I may not be as innocent as most girls, I know there are bad men out there, but to be thrown into the lion's den like this, I find the lump in my throat making it difficult to swallow.

Lifting my chin, I glance at him trying to formulate my response. My father has always taught me to fight. *Business is ruthless*, he told me. *Make sure you learn who your opponent is, and you'll be able to take them down easily.*

"What if I'm not innocent?" I bite out, but when he closes the distance between us, my body jolts as panic slams into me. He's ferocious when he glares at me, but he doesn't strike. He doesn't say anything, he just watches me. Dark eyes hold me hostage in their feral stare. As much as I see the rage in his gaze as if he's ready to rip me to pieces, he doesn't touch me. He just observes. Like a predator. Matching the wolf's mask that hides his face.

"Something tells me you are, little one." He smirks then and it has me wanting to see more of his face. He's beautifully built, almost perfectly so, and I imagine his face to be just as handsome. As if he can read my mind, he spins on his heel, lifting what looks like a whip from a hook on the wall and my stomach somersaults with anxiety.

"Are you going to take my virginity?" Words fall from my mouth unbidden, but the question stills him for a moment. His muscles tense in the T-shirt he's wearing and it looks like he's about to hulk out of it. He's not big, but the lean muscle is taut in his shoulders and back. His head drops, the movement makes me think he wants to answer, wants to do what I just asked. Once again, he's fighting between right and wrong.

"No, I'm not allowed to."

"That doesn't make sense. I've been stolen and brought to..." As my words taper off, I gesture around the darkened room, unsure of what to call it. A dungeon? A cellar? "I just need to know. What's going to happen to me?" My voice sounds almost childlike as I implore him to give me answers. Not the cryptic ones he's been feeding me so far.

Pulling the belt from his jeans, he reaches over and fastens it around my neck. "If you keep asking questions, I'm going to gag your pretty little mouth. It's best that you accept where you are. I'll only tell you what you need to know. It's safer for you." His warm breath fans over my face with a scent of coffee and mint. "Act like the perfect pet, and you'll be just fine."

I shiver as if I've been dunked in ice-cold water. I want to ask more questions, but instead I meet his eyes and nod. My lips are pursed tightly, but I'm dying to talk. All my life I've been told to speak up, ask questions. Being told the complete opposite is difficult for me to comprehend. I guess I am feisty. Which may have me ending up hurt, or worse.

Tears burn my eyes, but I refuse to let them fall. So I wait, my hands placed on my thighs hoping I'm coming across as submissive as he wants me to be.

For a moment, all he does is look at me. As if I'm a piece of art on display and he's trying to figure out what I mean. The pupils of his eyes dilate, even though the irises are dark, I can see the movement. It's hypnotic. Everything about this confuses me.

"I'm scared," I tell him honestly. I don't know why I'm trying to talk to him. Maybe to make him feel more human and less feral. He's got an animalistic aura, besides the mask, there's a rough edge to the deep rumble of his tone.

"I know, you should be." That's all he says before he tugs me along the floor and orders me to stand and bend over the large wooden table which sits against a concrete wall. There are whips, canes, and a few other things I don't know the name of hanging from silver hooks.

An array of objects to the right of where we are sit in perfect order on a side table. Silver, glinting in the dark light, shaped like an ace of spades which is found on playing cards. I've heard girls giggling about things like that, but have never seen them up close.

"Those are butt plugs," he speaks from behind me. I'm bent over, my eyes facing the wall in front of me, so I can't see what he's doing. There's no shuffle of material, so I know he's not moving around.

Anticipation tightens my belly with the fear of him hurting me with those silver things. *Butt plugs.* Even the name sounds like something that would hurt. Moving my head toward the left, I find another table, this one with bright pink, purple, and blue dildos. I know what they are since the girls at school told me about them.

I'm eighteen, still a virgin, but I know a few things about sex. I've just never had a boyfriend to even attempt it with. Moments pass in silence, but I've been in this position for what seems like hours. I want to once again say something, but my fear overrides the need to talk. Closing my eyes, I allow myself to relax into having my body bent at the waist. Suddenly, a harsh swat lands on my ass causing me to yelp.

"Don't make a noise, little one," he growls. There's a lilt in his voice that makes me hyper aware of the same tone I've heard before. When my father's associates used to come to the house and they'd talk to me. I didn't think anything of it until now.

I recognize it from the way Samael spoke to me only last night. It's desire. Pulling my lower lip between my teeth, I chew on it, hoping for salvation. Another swat and another land harshly on my ass. To keep from crying out, I bite down on my lip.

"So pretty. I want to see what you look like without panties," he murmurs, which has me jolting upright, spinning to face him. I shouldn't have done it because his eyes glower with anger. "Down!" he grunts and I immediately obey.

"Please, don't hurt me." The plea falls from my mouth, breathy and raspy. My stomach is tight with emotion that I don't understand. I'm in a constant state of confusion and fear, but also anticipation of what's coming next.

"I won't hurt you if you behave," he promises, to which I nod. I don't know if I can believe him, or if I can trust him, but I close my eyes and wait. He tugs my panties down my legs gently. It's such a complete contradiction of his earlier action that my knees buckle.

When he stops, my eyes snap open hoping to see what his next move is. I know he's going to use one of the toys on me. Leaving my underwear at my knees, he moves around to the small table on the left of me and picks up a small white tube.

Questions burn my throat, unease settles heavily in my stomach. I hear the click of the lid and tears once again threaten. I'm bare to him. To his gaze. I feel it burning a hole through me, then the cold liquid drips onto my ass.

A tremble skitters down my spine. His fingers trace lines over the skin of my ass while he massages the cream into the burning flesh. "You have incredible skin, Paige," he murmurs my name and somehow, it warms me.

His fingers dart between my legs, stroking the place no other man has touched before and I can't stifle my shocked gasp at the feeling. It doesn't hurt. Heat pools in my belly, but my mind races with how wrong this is. Why is my body responding? Why am I enjoying the way his fingers tease the flesh?

"You need to shave, little one." His words have the effect I needed to stop my traitorous body. They douse me in ice water, straight into my veins.

"I-I... I've never—"

"I'll have one of the other girls help you." That's all he says before pulling my panties back up. He tugs the leash allowing me to stand. "I'm taking you back to your room. You need to rest. Tomorrow we start your training."

FOUR

Kael

ONCE I GET BACK TO MY ROOM, MY HEAD IS SPINNING WITH what happened. I should still be in that room, showing her how to take a spanking, but I can't. Her body, her scent, everything is like a drug shot into my veins.

I don't know how I'm going to train her when all I want to do is fuck her. Those beautiful pink lips that glistened when I stroked her were almost my undoing. Her cunt is incredible. I'd never been so hard while training a pet before.

I don't understand it. Yes, I think she's beautiful, but as much as I should be taking her straight into the deep end and showing her how harsh this life is, I find myself wanting to make her mine instead.

Her fire, that intense sass that she throws my way mixed with the sweet innocence of sex is so different to the other toys I've had. Granted, most of them are virgins, but none were this addictive. As soon as I left her in her room, I wanted to go right back and see her again.

The door to my bedroom flies open and my brother stalks in. "Dad wants to see you," he smirks. The eyes of a wolf pierce me with venom, which I return tenfold.

"I'll be there in a minute."

"How was your little redhead? Isn't she...invigorating?" He breathes the word sensually. As if he's attempting to entice a beautiful woman into his bed. However, that would be easy for him.

"She's a good girl." I offer my response as I push off the bed and stalk toward him. We both step out into the hallway heading to my father's office.

"How long will it take you to break her?"

Shrugging, I try to play it off like it doesn't mean anything, but deep down, I know I'm only lying to myself. She's gotten under my skin and I've only spent a short time with her. What I'm going to have to do now is forget any feelings that she's stirred up and focus on work. On shattering the beautiful bird and watching her fall from the sky.

"Kael, you do realize she's only here to dance, to make Dad money." My brother's words break through the worrying thoughts in my mind and I nod.

"I know. Give me two weeks, she'll break." Even as I utter the words, they taste like lies on my tongue. Meeting the blue eyes of Samael Wolfe, I smirk, hoping for once my brother can't see under the mask I fake for him.

"Good, I reckon it will take you much longer. I say a month. Put your money where your mouth is and we'll have some fun."

He leaves me at the door to my father's office and saunters off dressed in his signature black suit. The man looks like he belongs in a boardroom rather than in this godforsaken place. Twisting the doorknob, I push into my father's office to find him sitting behind his large desk. This room is dark and dreary, just like the man himself.

"Ah, Kael. Come in, son." He gestures to the chair, the same one I sat in when he told me I would start training. The day he took my life and flushed it down the drain along with my brother's.

"Sam said you wanted to see me?" He nods, glancing at the pages on the desk, then brings his blue eyes back to me. It's only Sam and Theia, my younger sister, who have his eyes. Mine are dark brown tinged with black. Sometimes I wonder if he's my father at all.

"This new girl you've got, Paige Madden, I want you to make sure she's ready for the rooms within a month," he says, leaning back in his chair like he's sitting on a throne. A dark king ruling over a nightmarish kingdom.

"A month? I-I... I don't think she's going to be—"

"Did I fucking ask you what you think?" he hisses, rising to full height, and placing both hands flat on the desk. His glare roots me in place. "I want her ready in a month. She'll start dancing as soon as possible. Her father owes me big time and I think the redhead will bring in some big cash."

My heart thuds in my chest, threatening to break through the bone, flesh, and fall at my feet in time for him to step on it. "But, Father—"

"If you question me, I'll give her to Sam. Do you understand me? I'll be keeping a close eye on you. That little whore will try to coax you, she's a fucking temptress. Under no circumstances are you to form a bond. I don't care if you're my son, I'll end you."

His eyes burn with a white-hot anger that threatens to burn me alive. I don't doubt the man is capable of murdering his own flesh and blood. "One month," I confirm, pushing up, I head to the door. I can feel the heat of his glower on my back, but I don't turn around, I don't show weakness.

My father is a predator and when he smells fear, he attacks.

Making my way back to my bedroom, I consider going to see her. I know I shouldn't, he's just warned me, my mind is telling me to be careful, but the need I have for her is telling me to throw caution to the wind.

I would, but putting her in danger is not something I can allow myself to do. So, I turn and head away from the quarters where the girls live and straight for my bedroom. The sun is gone and the stars have already started to light the sky.

Pulling out my phone, I hit dial on Theia's number. Like I could have predicted she answers on the second ring. "Kael!"

"Theia, I need your help with something. Please, little Wolfe."
I smile when she huffs in response to the nickname I've given her.

"Anything for you, as long as you quit calling me that." Her retort is playful, our banter has always been easy. She's four years my junior, but sometimes I think she's older. Having had to grow up too soon. "And if it has anything to do with your new girl, I overheard Dad asking Dax to keep an eye on her." Her words are like ice water to my veins. If he's got Dax on guard duty then he must know something we don't. Or, he's noticed my tension when he mentioned her earlier.

"I need you to get Scarlett to help Paige. She needs to be shaven, clean." I don't have to explain further because my sister knows exactly what the clients want.

A soft sigh on the other end of the line tells me she's about as happy with this as I am. Every time we get a new girl it's the same thing. "Okay, Kael. I'll talk to you later." She hangs up before I have time to thank her, but I know she's miserable here and I don't blame her. I hope she'll get out. Soon.

I settle on my bed and grab a book hoping I can read to focus my mind on anything but the beauty that's lying in her bed alone and scared. The one I want to save. Only, I don't know how.

Rousing from a dream-filled sleep, I roll over to glance at the time. It's early, the sun hasn't even risen yet and I've been dreaming of a redhead. I stare for too long at the geometric patterns in the ceiling, trying to make out the way the lines come to each other in a puzzle. The dim light in the room from the full moon casts a silver glow on the darkened bedding and furnishings.

My room is my only haven. The one place I can escape what happens in this house. It's a new day and time for me to take my pet to play. Today she'll learn more than what my hand feels like on her ass. I want to see her squirm in pleasure, hear her moan in delight, and taste her when she unravels. And I know just the way to do it. Heading into the bathroom, I turn on the shower and wait for it to heat until it's scalding. Stripping off, I step under the spray and hiss at the burn on my skin.

I grab the shower gel and lather up quickly. I want to get breakfast out of the way before the sun is up because I want to get to her room early. I want to spend the day with her. To torture her with pleasure. I'm so far gone. Shaking my head, I rinse off and shut off the taps.

Moments later I'm dressed in a pair of ripped black jeans and a white T-shirt. My usual get up for training. Only this time, the black hoodie I regularly wear lies discarded on the bed.

With only my mask in hand, I make my way down to the kitchen to grab something to eat. Knowing the girls wouldn't have been fed yet, I plan on taking my new toy something. Upon reaching our humongous kitchen, I find Hesta.

"Hello, Kael," she offers with a friendly smile. She's never asked about anything more than she needed to know. Turning a blind eye might be wrong, but for her it's a matter of life and death. My father is ruthless.

"Good morning, Hesta." I lean in and plant a kiss on top of her head. "Has Samael come down yet?" She shakes her head and rolls her eyes. My brother loves sleeping in on the weekend.

"You know what he's like. What are you having today?"

"Can you make me one breakfast and I'll just have coffee for now." Her brows shoot up at my request. "It's for someone." She nods in understanding and sets about plating up some toast and frying the eggs. There's always food ready and waiting and this morning is no different.

As soon as the plate is stacked, I grab a mug of coffee and fill it setting it on the tray along with the rest of the breakfast. Before I walk out of the kitchen, Hesta meets my eyes with a worried stare. "Look after her, Kael."

I don't know how to respond, so I nod and make my way up to the bedroom that's been beckoning me like a damn siren's call all night.

FIVE

Paige

THE DOOR OPENS STARTLING ME AWAKE. WHEN I HEAR IT click closed, I roll over and peer at the man who's seemed to invade my mind all night. I don't know him. I have no idea why I can't get him off my mind, but I spent most of my night trying to figure out who he is.

"Good morning, Paige," he utters in that low gravelly tone. He's either just woken up, or he's been smoking. I doubt it's the latter since the scent of his cologne wafts around him like an intoxicating fog.

I don't respond immediately. I watch him set the tray on a table against the wall opposite the bed. He doesn't ask me to talk to him or even greet him. His body moves to the small radio on the dresser and he turns it on.

A song filters through the room and I recognize it. "Nights Like This" by W. Darling. A small smile plays on my lips at his choice of music. "I don't really listen to this type of music," he rumbles grumpily. "I figured since you're a young girl you'd like it and it would perhaps set you at ease."

"How could I be at ease when I've been stolen? Nothing would make it okay. Don't you understand?" As always, my words are fiery, but all he does is stare at me for a moment.

"No, it's not okay. But, if you're going to act like an insolent pet then I'll treat you like one. You need to eat to gain some strength for what I have planned today. I can't have you passing out, Firebird." He turns and heads for the door and for some reason, I feel bad for snapping at him. It doesn't make sense. But I can't help calling out to him.

"Wait!" He stops and glances at me again. "You've decided to give me a name, but what do I call you?" I question.

"You can call me Wolfe."

With that, I'm left alone. *Wolfe.* I tease the name on my lips. My father's partner's last name is Wolfe. His son had a mask on which resembled a wolf's face. *Are they family?* Or is this part of the charade. I've overheard some of the girls talk about clients with masks. But if they're all family, what does that make my Wolfe? *Is he also Harlan's son?* Thoughts drift in and out as my mind plays out all the intricacies. My stomach rumbling is the only sign I have that I need to eat.

Nothing about this makes any sense. If he is Harlan's son, then why is he doing this? Surely my father would know if they'd taken me. Unless my father's partner is hiding my disappearance. My heart bangs violently against my chest. That's the only reason

I can think of. The other that comes to mind is something I don't want to entertain at all. But somehow, my intuition tells me my father may be involved. I have nothing to go on, except my gut.

Pushing off the bed, I settle at the table and pick up the mug of coffee. His words replay in my mind. I need strength for today. A sliver of anxiety shoots through me and I pray he's not going to hurt me badly.

I'm dressed in a pair of black yoga pants and a white tank top when Wolfe stalks into my room twenty minutes later. "Let's go," he grunts, but doesn't come near me to fasten a collar around my neck.

Strangely, it makes me smile that he's not treating me like a dog today. We walk in silence to the room he brought me to yesterday. The same room where he bent me over a table and touched me between my thighs.

Last night a pretty brunette, who said her name is Scarlett, came to my room and helped me shave myself where Wolfe had touched me. It was as humiliating as I thought it would be. She was gentle and kind, and I immediately wanted to ask her more questions, but as soon as I spoke about Sam or what happens in this place she shut down.

"Get inside," he grunts when we stop at the open door. Stumbling into the room, I glance around and find it's in darkness except for a few large candles. "On your knees. I want your eyes on the floor, your hands will be placed on your thighs palms up."

His orders come swiftly, efficiently, and I notice he's closed off. The emotion that was there yesterday has gone, it's been replaced with a cold exterior. Perhaps I can find it by playing by his rules.

My mind races with thoughts of how I can make him soften toward me. If he cares, maybe he'll free me. A plan slowly formulates in my mind as I stare at the concrete. "If you talk out of turn, I will whip you. Should you decide not to obey me, I'll punish you. Today you'll learn to take a whip. Tomorrow, the cane," he informs me with a rigid grunt.

I don't respond.

I don't move.

His footfalls near me after the door shuts with a resounding click. When his shoes appear in my line of sight, I wait. He still doesn't touch me, but I feel his eyes. They roam my skin like a burning flame. Frowning at the emotions stirring inside me, I shut my eyes trying to will away the tingle of anticipation.

I shouldn't want this. But he's eased the fear, leaving me confused. "Look at me," he orders. I lift my eyes and meet his dark ones. "I want you to rise, without using your hands on the floor. Foot by foot." Easily, I rise, stepping on my right foot first, then my left. "Good girl," he coos causing my stomach to somersault.

He lifts the collar I didn't notice him holding and fastens it around my neck.

"I want you kneeling on the bench, take off that top and

those pants. I want you naked. And as always when we're in here, no words. You obey me. And you'll be rewarded." Shock has my mouth falling open, but I'm not sure how badly he'll hurt me if I speak, so with my eyes brimming with unshed tears, I make quick work of undressing. I head over to the leather bench. There are three parts to it. Allowing my torso to comfortably rest on the center panel with my legs and arms on either side. Without speaking, he fastens my ankles, then my wrists.

His touch is firm, yet gentle. It's warm, yet icy cold. When silence falls once more, I can't help the dread weighing heavily in my gut. Then I hear a swish. The sound is so gentle, but I know the sting will be harsh.

"Remember to be silent, little one." Before I have time to acknowledge him the leather bites into the skin of my ass causing me to whimper. "I told you to be quiet. It's difficult, but you'll learn." His anger silences me immediately. Another swish, another sting, it continues until tears are streaming down my cheeks.

It's silent when the lashes finally stop. My body's vibrating in agony, yet my mind feels as if I'm looking down on myself. Like I'm having an out of body experience. The cuffs fall away from my wrists and ankles. Suddenly cold liquid trickles over my inflamed skin.

His hands rough, his touch gentle as he rubs the soothing balm over my ass. "You'll be in pain for a day, tomorrow our training will start later so you have time to recover. I've been gentle with you, Firebird. Next time I won't be able to hold back."

No other words are spoken as he allows me to dress. There's a silent rage that surrounds him. I don't know if it's because of what he just did, or if he's angry with me. When I glance at him, I notice his gaze trained on the wall. His hands fist and release at his sides, then those dark orbs turn to me, pinning me with a heated stare.

"It's best you get used to the pain," he murmurs then, his voice rough with emotion, only I can't pinpoint what it is. Guilt and anguish are at the forefront, but there's a hunger in his tone. Dropping my eyes to his jeans I notice the bulge that's prominent behind his zipper.

"You like hurting me?" I question, my voice soft and croaky from crying. He stares at me a moment longer before turning away.

"It's my job." That's all he utters before he escorts me back to my room, this time on my hands and knees collared like a pet. He doesn't say goodbye, he doesn't even look at me before leaving me on my bed alone with tears still racing down my cheeks.

I'll Always Covet You

To covet the forbidden is dangerous,
Yet, I see no threat in your eyes
When you look in mine
All you'll see is love

SIX

Paige

A WEEK. I'VE BEEN HERE FOR SEVEN DAYS. EACH MORNING he comes to me, I count. And each time the door opens I can't wait to look at him. To see his eyes, his face. The slight scruff that dusts his chin.

"Paige," he murmurs this morning in his gruff tone.

"Wolfe," I respond quietly. As usual, he leaves my breakfast on the table and turns to walk away. I think he's leaving, but he stops at the dresser and settles in the chair. He drags his dark eyes over to me, taking me in. "Are you going to take me now?"

The question falls from my lips before I have time to think. I'm shocked when he laughs. It's a rumbling sound which makes me smile. I find myself wanting to hear it again as soon as it stops.

"I don't take, Paige. When I'm with a woman it's because she's begging for it." His confidence hangs heavy in the air, but his words have jealousy swirling around in my belly. I don't want to feel something for him, but I can't deny I do. "Besides you don't want me to fuck you, Firebird. Because I won't be gentle. It will hurt and you'll cry, and you know what?" I shake my head, my mouth dry as the fucking desert because fear races through me. My mind is blank with what to say, but I don't get a chance to respond because he answers for me. "I'll enjoy every moment of seeing your tight little cunt opening like a flower as it swallows my cock."

"You have a filthy mouth," I retort. All my life, I've been spoken to with respect, like I'm a prim and proper princess. Now, as this savage man who would love to inflict pleasured pain on me utters such filthy words, I find myself aching for him to show me exactly what he means. He doesn't know he's playing right into my hands. The only way I'll get out of here is to make the monster feel.

"And you have a feisty little mouth. One that I'd like to shove my cock down and watch as you swallow it," he taunts. His voice is low, gravely, and I know he's as turned on as I am.

"Then why don't you show me?" He rises from the chair, stalks toward me on the bed, and leans in. Hot breath with the scent of coffee whispers over my face. Lifting my chin, I meet his intense stare. He grips my chin between his thumb and index finger.

His mouth is so close to mine, if I moved an inch, I'd be able to taste him, to feel his lips mold to mine. But I don't. I wait. His tongue darts out, licking the seam of my lips. A deep rumble vibrates in his chest. He grips my hair at the nape of my neck and tugs me impossibly closer, as if he's trying to climb inside me. "You taste so sweet, little one," he murmurs almost reverently.

"Do I get to taste you, Sir?" I breathe the word, which has his smirk returning full force, and I can't help smiling. His eyes flit between my lips and my eyes. But when they settle on my deep green pools, he nods.

"You really want this?" he questions, and I nod. "If I took your mouth now, if I claimed it as mine, you'd allow me to? Because, as much as I do this shit, I don't force myself on any woman. So you'll need to beg."

His eyes that peek at me through his mask bleed with sincerity. "Would you like it if I begged?" My sassy remark grants me another tug on the strands he has in a fierce grip.

"I'd fucking love it, Firebird. To hear you whimper my name as I rain down swats on your beautiful ass while I'm deep inside you would be the ultimate heaven. Even though this isn't the life I chose for myself, deep down, I love the control." The more he speaks, the more my skin heats. As he utters his desires, my own tumble and twist low in my core, tugging at me. "I love to mark you. But I won't make you do something you don't want to. Your strength when we're in there does things to me. Things that are forbidden. I shouldn't want you this much, Paige." The room feels too small. He's too close. My body is too aware of how much I want him. I shiver at the words he utters. Reaching up, I run a finger over the strike of red that marks the left side of his mask.

"Why?" I ask quietly.

"Because if they know I do, they'll kill me and you." My heart leaps into my throat at his brutally honest confession. This isn't something he should be sharing. "My heart isn't what you see within these walls, Firebird."

"Why do you stay? And why call me firebird?"

"I stay because it's my prison. And you my little one are as rare as a bird born of fire, and as beautiful as one too." His thumb swipes over my lips, with his gaze penetrating me in such a way I feel naked. His touch scorches me. This is a part of him. He's opening up to me, allowing me to see behind the façade.

And even though he's still wearing a mask, he's showing me a glimpse into his heart. In the darkness of the world we've been thrown into, I see light. Because I see him. He leans in further, warm lips on mine. "You look at me too closely," he mumbles against my lips. His mouth hovers lightly over mine. It sends a jolt of desire shooting through me, and I wish he'd just devour me.

"You make me feel like you want me to. I see you, Wolfe."

He smiles at my words, and it's a sight to behold. I wish I could see his whole face—to get the full effect of his beauty—but what I have to work with has to be enough.

"Perhaps I do want you to see me. The real me." He ghosts the words along my lips, and then he does it. His mouth finally molds to mine. The heat of his kiss, the scruff on his chin, his body pressing against mine, everything turns me molten. Need burns like a flame in my belly. My hands come up, twining around his neck and pulling him closer. The ridge of his erection presses against my stomach, I hum my approval as my hips rise. Needing the friction, the heat, the touch.

Our tongues duel, our bodies burn, mine alight with a yearning that tightens everything below my belly button. His hands grip my hips painfully, as if he's trying to mold his body to mine.

When we finally break the kiss, my lips are hot, swollen, and wet. My tongue wants to taste him again. "You're a temptress, Firebird."

"And you're a sinful seducer, Wolfe. I've never... I mean, I don't..." My words taper off, but seem to halt his movements. He slowly releases my hip where his one hand had found purchase during the kiss.

"What, Paige?" he questions, his voice still husky with desire. "I know you're a virgin, it's obvious, but don't tell me you've never been kissed."

"I've been kissed before, but I've never been consumed by a man like that." My voice is barely audible, but he's close enough to hear me. The corner of his mouth lifts into a sinful smirk.

"Somehow, with those big green eyes and your delicious body, I don't think it will be the last," he utters. I think I hear jealousy dripping from the words, but I can't be sure. At least, I don't think it would be wise for us to even journey down this path. He told me I'm forbidden, and as much as I want to stick to my plan, to make him care, I fear I'm the one falling.

Lifting my gaze to his, I lean forward. "Will you do it again?" Hope fills my chest and it laces my words. A blush spreads across my cheeks at the question, and I feel immature for asking.

"You're going to be the death of me, little one," he vows in a tone filled with barely restrained hunger and agony. As if wanting me hurts him. I suppose it does since he's not allowed to.

"Tell me why you're so scared of letting go," I question, acting braver than I feel. A shudder that travels over my body is evidence of my apprehension. He moves off me completely, standing at full height.

"Sit back," he orders and I scoot against the headboard. Watching him curiously, I can't help smiling when he settles beside me. Immediately, I feel his warmth and affection. *This man isn't a monster.*

"If I do let go with you, I'll hurt you. I... There are things I like, things I enjoy, and I don't want you to see that kind of darkness. The darkness that runs through my veins. Yes, I've whipped you, and I've caned you, but that's my job." His words still me, squeezing my heart. There's a certain sadness in his voice, causing me to turn to him fully. I'm on my knees gazing at him. I want to know more about him. I want to delve inside his mind, to learn about who he is, what his dreams are and how they differ from mine. He continues then, telling me with a smirk, "For me, I enjoy other ways of delicious torture."

"You won't hurt me." The surety in my tone startles us both. Something shifts between us. Emotion passes from me to him, as if a rope is tethering my heart to his. Because when he glances at me again, meeting my stare head on, I see it. Affection. He cares for me. He might not want to. But he does.

"You shouldn't believe that," he says earnestly.

"Well, I do." Pushing up, I rise to stand beside the bed, my arms crossed over my chest, causing him to chuckle. He swings his legs over the edge, his hands grip my hips and he pulls me closer, so I'm positioned between his thighs. For the first time, I'm staring down at him, and him up at me.

"You're a little firecracker, and you're going to burn me alive. Aren't you?" he asks. His smile is incredible, it lights his dark eyes reminding me of dark chocolate. Nodding, I place my hands on his shoulders and feel the tension ease at my touch.

"Tell me why you're here, if this isn't what you want. And why do I scare you so much?" For a beat, he just watches me. Our connection strengthens with every thud of my heart, and when I shift my thumb, I feel the thrum of his pulse just below the smooth skin of his neck.

"You ask too many questions, baby." The word falls from his mouth—it tumbles and hangs between us. My heart kicks in my chest at the endearment, and our gazes lock.

"And you evade too many answers," I respond quietly, my

voice low as I lean in closer, inhaling his scent. Spicy, warm, and it reminds me of cinnamon and cigars. A smoky sweetness. It's just him.

"If I tell you about me, it makes this personal. It drags you into my darkness, and I fear your light will be dimmed, Firebird," he murmurs against my cheek.

"What if I scorched your darkness and let it burn to ash?" I feel his smile against my skin, and it sends goosebumps rising all over my body.

"Then perhaps we'll rise from those very ashes, baby." A cocky smirk on his lips has me grinning.

"Aren't you the poetic one?"

"Don't get used to it. I'm not always this lyrical." He chuckles, and I can't help feeling happiness ease itself between us. It's a foreign feeling after the week of torment, and I know as soon as the next words are out of my mouth, I'm going to regret asking them.

"Do you know why I was kidnapped?" The gates shut in his eyes, turning his face to stone. The icy chill of his demeanor sends a shudder through me.

"I told you, little firebird, you ask too many questions." With that, he rises, leaving me on my bed. "I'll be back later. Be dressed. I'm taking you into room five for training." He opens the door, and when it shuts behind him, tears break the barrier and stream down my face.

I fucked it up. We were getting somewhere, and I had to go open my big mouth. This morning I overheard a couple of the other girls talking. Apparently, room five is the worst one, filled with toys that hurt. Not the pleasurable hurt, but the kind of pain that will stay with me. He must be angry. I wonder if he's angry at me for asking the questions, or at himself for not being able to give me the answers.

SEVEN

Kael

SHE ASKED QUESTIONS I COULDN'T ANSWER. EVEN THOUGH I want to give them all to her. The way she looks at me with those emerald pools that disarm me. That kiss, her touch, everything seems to be churning in my gut like a storm brewing within me. I'm caught up in her magic. In her flames. And I'm going to get burned.

This is no life for someone like her. For any of the girls here, but Paige is different. Special. I'd love to take her outside so I can see the rays of sunlight brighten her eyes. To watch her hair come alive like dancing flames that remind me of the fire that rages in her eyes. Everything about this woman has consumed me.

I'm going to die in her blaze and I can't do anything about it. Not because I don't want to, but because I'm already falling. And if it means I'm burned alive, then so be it.

If my father finds out about us, about these feelings, he'll not only torture Paige, he'll make sure she shatters. And he'll enjoy every moment. He'll take the one thing I know he's dying to claim. Her purity. The only reason he hasn't done it yet is because his clients prefer virgins. And he gets paid more.

The thought of any other man touching her sends jealousy coursing through me, and rage burning in my veins. Even though I have no say over it as I know I'm going to have to let go soon.

If I could save her I would. All I can do is make sure she's ready for the moment she steps into those vile rooms. Where there's no light left. Only darkness and depravity. I can't be her prince, but I'll be her knight. Not the one she wanted, but I'm the only one she's going to get. It kills me not to be able to really talk to her. To explain why my life is spent in this godforsaken place—because no God would step foot inside here.

Shame haunts me daily, guilt riddles my veins—it slowly eats at me, and I'm left with nothing. Just a shell. I don't want this. I've never wanted to be like my father, but I have no choice. If I try to leave, he'll kill me. His own son. Unless...

"Kael!" My sister's happy tone comes from behind me. I turn to find the little pixie almost floating on her pink ballet flats. She regards me with a wide grin.

"What's got you so happy, Theia?"

"Dad's agreed to allow me to work full time with Dax. Well, at his club. Since it's nothing like Caged, you know Dad doesn't give a fuck about it. And the agreement Dax has with Daddy Dearest is that Inferno is his alone. So I'll be moving out. Inferno has apartments above the club, so I'll only be here when I'm needed. Which I'm hoping is never."

Nodding, I pull her into my arms. My sister is the only other woman in my life that I can't help allowing into my darkened heart. She brings light, just like Paige. "I'm happy for you. This life is not something you should be caught up in."

"It's definitely not my idea of quality family time, that's for sure." She pouts, scrunching her nose.

"You're lucky," I tell her honestly. When I meet her gaze, I know she can see how I feel. The hurt, the pain from being in here. It's too much. So fucking much.

"You'll get out. One day. Perhaps with some beautiful woman you'll fall hopelessly in love with and you two will live happily ever after." She giggles playfully.

That's one thing about my sister, she's a nosy little wench sometimes. Even though I shouldn't say anything, I nod. "Maybe."

"I better get going. I love you, brother." A quick peck on the cheek, and my little sister bounds off, probably to find Dax.

I head up to my suite, needing the silence of the room to calm me. Especially from the woman who's invaded my mind. I've never found it difficult to separate feelings and emotions from what I do. I learned how to block them out, but Paige has found a crack in my shield and she's burrowed herself in there without me realizing it until only moments ago.

There's strength in her, which is good because it's the only thing that will get her out of here. If something happens to me, I hope Samael will look after her. Perhaps not like I can, but in his own way.

My brother is an asshole, but not a day goes by that I don't hope and pray to anyone who will listen that Sam finds love. He's cold, shut off—it's his coping mechanism to be an asshole. It's the only way he knows how to survive this life we've been thrown into. I think, deep down, he needs a woman who can not only push his boundaries, but to take what he can offer. Only then will my brother be happy.

Settling myself in front of my computer, I pull up the browser I had open the other day. A gallery in New York looking for artists. My heart lies there, but ever since Paige, it lies here too. I want to break her out of here and steal her away.

Can I do it? Is a normal life possible for her and me?

There's no doubt I'll be hers. But will she be mine? Will she be able to let go of the anger I see in her eyes and just believe this is something I have no choice in?

Questions. That's all I have. It's all I can focus on because the answers I need are not within reach. Not yet, anyway. The need to run is at the forefront of my mind. To throw Paige in the car and drive through the gates of our estate, to leave this place without looking back. But I can't. I'll be caught before I even reach them.

It's not only the girls who are held here. In some fucked up way, Sam and I are also held by the prison my father has set for us.

My heart hurts for us. The two Wolfe boys, brought into a

blue-blooded family. One of the sickest families in the country.

Shaking my head, I continue my search and pour over pages consisting of apartments I'll never have. Places I'll never visit with her. With my firebird.

I've always dreamed of a family. Children. When I look at her now, I ache to see her swollen with my child. Perhaps two.

Before the thoughts drag me under, I shove away from my desk. Heading into the bathroom, I strip down and turn on the tap. The cascading water turns from an ice-cold waterfall to scorching rain, and I step under the scalding shower. With my eyes shut, I picture her. Her beautiful curves, her long flowing hair, those lips. Fuck, those lips.

Her small, delicate hands. Long, lithe legs. Beautiful, creamy skin I want to lick every inch of. Fuck, I need her. Fisting my dick, I picture her bound by crimson rope. I'd like to have her tied, open to me. Her tight body needy for me as she begs. Calls me Sir.

My hand moves faster as I imagine sliding into her cunt. Into her tight ass. Owning every fucking hole. My head falls back as my balls tighten, pulling up with my release. Growling her name as I find my temporary bliss, I make my vow under the water that's attempting to cleanse me.

She's mine. I'll have her.

And I'll make sure she never forgets me. Whatever happens.

TO BURN IN YOUR BLAZE

Anger, violence, and hatred
Emotions that fuel you
Pleasure, tenderness, and love
Emotions that burn me
And I'd gladly turn to ash because of you

EIGHT

Paige

I'VE BEEN ALONE IN MY BEDROOM FOR THREE MORNINGS. Scarlett brought my breakfast each day, but she didn't stay long. I don't leave the bedroom unless he's with me. And I don't know when I'll see him again.

The room itself isn't bad. The queen-sized bed is pretty with white sheets and a crimson comforter. There's only one window which is too high for me to see out of, but there's a sky light which wakes me when morning comes.

An en suite bathroom with a large shower and bath sits to the left of my bed. There's not much else in the room besides the table and dresser. A small closet just beside it. All the furnishings are a dark red, almost the color of blood. There's black and silver that pop against the walls that are painted an off white—with no art, no clocks, nothing, they're bare, just like me.

After Wolfe left me three days ago, I spent the night staring at the stars through my skylight. It was last night after sleep stole me that I dreamt of the night of my eighteenth birthday. It was a memory which forced itself into my mind and now, as I lie here, I try to recall it.

Turning on the little stereo, the iPod shuffles and a song comes on, slamming me back in time. Just over a week ago. The night of the masked ball. My birthday. The day my whole life changed.

"Paige, I would like to see you in my office. You head down and I'll be there soon." My father smiles, but his face is tense with emotion.

Nodding, I give him a few moments, grabbing another glass of champagne, draining it. I close my eyes, enjoying the bubbles as they fizzle their way down my throat. Once I've set the glass on a passing waiter's silver tray, I head down the hallway toward the large room he uses as his home office. It's more like a study, with shelves of books and a large fireplace. The memory of the kiss I've just had still has my body buzzing along with the alcohol that races through my bloodstream. Heat. His lips. His hands.

Shaking my head, I step in through the doorway and find myself alone. The party is in full swing, so I wonder why my father would call me away. Surely, he could have waited to talk to me tomorrow.

"Father?" I call out, but I'm met with silence. Reaching for the lamp on his desk, I turn it on. A low yellow light bathes the room with ghosts and shadows, and a cold shiver runs through me. Our home, though immaculate, is cold. It's always been devoid of love and emotion. My parents aren't the loving, cuddly kind. They expect me to be the poised doll, smiling at people I don't know and acting as the sweet and innocent woman. All in an effort to make my father look good under the public's

scrutiny. A family man. Nothing could be further from the truth. As much as I love him, we've never had a close relationship. I've always been a business transaction, nothing more.

A sound from behind startles me, and in the shadows, stands a figure. "Daddy?" I question while making my way toward him. He's silent, just watching. As if a scene is about to unfold, and he's entranced. As I reach him, his face is filled with remorse. His mouth moves, but he doesn't voice any words. Before I can say anything, my mouth is covered, and when I inhale a deep, shuddering breath, my eyes flutter closed and sleep beckons. Strong hands. An acrid smell.

And that's the last time I saw my father.

When my mind flits back to the present, I realize I should be getting dressed. Pushing up, I pad into the bathroom and freshen up. I need time to think, but I know I don't have any. He will be here soon, and I want to please him. The last time I saw him we had more time to bond and I can see he cares. Perhaps I can ask him about getting out of here.

I broke through to him, I saw the human side of the animal he hides behind. Aside from the orders he barks, he's always been silent and predatory. But I finally got him to open up to me. To give me more than just a grunted command.

The control and confidence he oozes, though, is intoxicating. We're in our second week of what he calls training. Slowly he's eased my fear, gotten under my skin. Even so, every time he shows me affection, it's as if he realizes his mistake and shuts down.

Something about him has me intrigued. Emotions surround this man like a hurricane—swirling with darkness and danger—anger, guilt, frustration, and one I didn't expect, desire.

"Paige," his gruff tone calls from the bedroom. When I step out wrapped in only my robe and a pair of panties beneath, I find him, masked, with nothing but a pair of jeans on. His skin is flawless, beautiful. No tattoos, no scars. "Are you ready?" His deep brown eyes rake over me, teasing me with a devious look.

"Yes, Sir," I murmur, and I swear I see him smirk.

"Good. I'd like to take you over to the room, for a little bit. Just... I need to spend some time in there," he murmurs. It's not an order, more like a request. As if he's asking rather than telling. His body is taut, muscles strained.

"Is this going to be a punishment?" I question. My curiosity is piqued when he turns to me. Dark eyes penetrate my very being, as if he's communicating his answer with a single glare. He allows me a moment to close the distance between us. When I reach for his face, his hand comes out, gripping my wrist to stop me.

"Don't touch my face. Please." His request is almost pained and it tugs at my heart.

"Why? I want to feel you. I want..." My words taper off when he pins me with a heated glower. My mouth hangs open, wondering if I should continue or not.

"Tell me," he orders with a sigh of frustration. I shut my mouth, take a deep breath and watch him, steeling myself before

I tell him the words I've wanted to since we kissed three days ago.

Shrugging, I moisten my lips and his gaze falls to my lips. "I want you." We stare at each other for so long, too long, in fact. We've never had sex. I'm still a virgin, but my ache for this man is intense. My body tingles, my skin heats, the quiver between my thighs awakens when his tongue moistens his lips.

When he's near me, I'm zapped with electric currents so fierce, it steals my breath. And I don't know how else to explain it, but I'm falling down the rabbit hole and there's no hope for me. I'm his. I've been his since I first laid eyes on him.

"You can't have me, Paige. I'm forbidden."

"As am I. But will that stop you?"

"Why do you taunt me?"

"I covet you, Wolfe. I want you to want me as much as I want you. There's no doubt in my mind." My response is quick—it earns me a ragged breath and a deep growl. "Please, take me." He glares at me then. His hands grip my hips and he carries me to my bed, lying me down. He reaches in his back pocket for the blindfold and hands it to me.

"Put that on," he orders, and I comply. Once my eyes are covered, I wait. For a moment, I think he's just playing with me. That he's teasing me by watching me lie in agony. But then I feel it. The belt of my robe is undone and then I'm mostly naked to his hungry gaze.

My body trembles, but not from cold, from the pure lust that races through me. Suddenly, I'm consumed by his mouth, I'm worshipped by his hands. They're all over me. As if he's trying to memorize every inch of my skin. Starting at my neck, he kisses me and devours me. His lips hot, his hands electric as they stroke the skin that's bare to him.

His tongue tastes, his lips consume, his growl is low and seductive, like he's been starving for so long and he's finally been fed a five-course meal. Slowly he moves down my body as my back arches off the bed, but his hands firmly hold my hips down until the hot breath from his full lips reaches my core.

When he releases me, I whimper at the loss of him, but a soft noise alerts me that he's moving. Then he gently splays my thighs to his gaze—at least, that's what I assume he's doing—and I realize I know why he asked me to wear the blindfold. He's taken his mask off.

I cry out when I feel him rip the panties from my hips, and his mouth crashes down on my pussy. I'm wet, drenched, and his tongue darts into the slick folds of my entrance.

"Jesus, Paige. Your cunt is decadent," he growls against the quivering flesh. "I could eat you all fucking day and never tire of you." I'm lost to the ecstasy that's racing through every inch of my body, trickling over every inch of my skin and squeezing the heart that's beating wildly in my chest for him.

"Please, I need you. I want your filthy mouth on me," I moan. I just want him to take me and make me his. Only his.

"Sassy little firebird," he grunts against my pussy. His fingers tease me open, and I know he's staring at me because I can feel my skin being scorched by his gaze. His lips latch on to my clit and he suckles it into his mouth. His teeth latch on, biting down hard, sending pure, pained pleasure shooting through every nerve in my body. My back arches off the bed again and this time he lets me ride out the bliss.

My fingers fist in his hair, and I tug him closer, needing more. Wanting him to fill me, but he doesn't. His tongue fucks my core, fast, hard, and deep, and then his fingers slide into me. Only deep enough to feel my resistance, which I'll gladly give him, but he doesn't take it. Instead, he pulls my hardened nub into his mouth again, pumping his fingers into my body.

"Come for me," he growls.

And I do. My body convulses and pulses around his digits, and this man, who is on his knees before me, drinks every drop of my release.

After I'd come down from my high, he made sure I was okay, and then left without so much as a word. I sat alone and confused for most of the day until he walked back into my room—mask firmly in place—blindfolded me again, and ordered me to follow with him tugging my leash.

He'd just brought me into the room where we normally train. When he ripped off the material covering my eyes moments ago, he didn't look directly at me, but rather at my wrists. "Why?" I beg, my voice sounding small and faint. "Just answer me?" Once again, he doesn't meet my questioning gaze. I thought he was about to say something when he turned to work the straps on a leather bench before me.

My anxiety calmed somewhat as he continued whatever it was he was doing. My mouth, however, was on automatic, needing to know what was going on. I needed to make him see we're right together. That we work. I know he'd be able to get me out of here. My plan failed, though. I wanted to make him love me, but I'm the one who's fallen. I really need him to show me his face, but what I want more is for him to show me his heart.

He's so silent, so closed off, I'm not sure if he regrets what happened earlier. Frustration burns in my gut, anxiety squeezes my heart, and I'm left with nothing but a man who can't give me an answer.

For the first time since we walked into this room he turns to me and I startle. "Look, I—" My words break off as his hand finds its way around my throat. The collar and his grasp tighten painfully, and stars begin to flicker in my vision.

"Shut. Up." His voice is thick, not with anger, though. Instead with...fear? "I can't do this if you're going to keep talking. Please, Firebird." For the first time since he made me come on his tongue he looks me dead in the eye, and I see it. That thing he's been trying to hide, but no longer can, because I can see it reflecting in his soul through his heated gaze. Affection.

As much as he'd like me to believe his soul is black, I know it's a lie. He's hurting as much as I am. "Well, if you're so fucking annoyed with me, why don't you hand me over to one of the others? Surely there's someone who'd like to play with me, seeing as you don't," I hiss as his grip tightens. His eyes glow. And I swear to all that's holy, it's as if there's a flame behind them.

"Do. Not. Test. Me," he growls, and my knees give way. Something about his tone and the way he's pressing me against the wall has a flood of heat rushing through me, settling with heaviness between my thighs.

"Why? Are you going to spank me?" I should shut up. I shouldn't push him. But my fiery personality and the fact that he's got my panties wet is more than I can handle. I should be scared. But I'm not. I'm more turned on than I've ever been.

Without a word, he pulls me forward, tugging me toward a bench that has leather and chains attached to it. My heart spikes, hammering against my ribs, deafening me. *Shit. What have I done?* "You want to be spanked? Huh?" he murmurs in my ear, and I find that deathly calm tone scarier than if he was shouting. My wrists are tugged forward, and I feel the thick cold leather before I see it. I'm bound, my arms stretched forward, my legs spread, and the cold metal around my ankles sends an icy shudder through me.

"What are you doing?" I whisper.

Suddenly, the mask is in front of me. "You are an insolent little pet. You need to be taught a lesson." He disappears from my line of sight, and then I feel it. Cold steel. Feathered lightly on my bare skin. The material of my underwear crumbles, and I try to turn my head, but it's no use. I can't see the blade. "So pretty. Your skin is like silk." His tone is raspy, needy.

"Please..."

Without a response or warning, a sharp sting bites down on my ass, and I yelp. Another joins it, left and right, again and again, and I'm wetter and more turned on than I was only moments ago. Than I've ever been. I've read about girls who get off on pain, but I never thought I could or would.

I may be a virgin, but I'm not naïve.

"Have you learned your lesson, or would you like more?" he says in my ear. The heat of his breath sends a tingle down my spine and hummingbirds flutter in my belly. My skin prickles with warmth, and my core pulses.

The heavy weight of his body doesn't move. He's waiting on an answer, and one falls from my lips without regret. "So much more," I whisper, and a feral growl rumbles in his chest, vibrating against me.

"Good girl."

Two words in his dark tone torment me. All I want is for him to take me. To show me pleasure—our flesh slapping against each other—but he doesn't. Instead, he moves away and proceeds to untie me. Pulling me up, he walks me over to the door, stopping short when it flies open and another man in a mask, this time one with a blue stripe adorning it, fills the space.

"You need to finish up. You're needed upstairs." My captor nods in response to the order. Rounding the stranger, whose voice I recognize as Samael, we head down the hallway. Once we're back in my bedroom, he turns to regard me.

"I'll be back for you later, Firebird," he grunts, leaving me reeling, needy, and confused.

"Firebird." His soft growl comes from behind me, and I roll over onto my back. Shuffling up against the headboard, I find my Wolfe. His dark gaze is primal. "Tonight, I want to take you into the VIP room where you can watch the stage without being seen. It will give you an idea of what is expected of you. As much as I don't want you to get into this, I don't have a choice." His words drip with affection and guilt. Two opposing emotions that shouldn't be felt together, but he always emanates both. He regards me with apology in those deep brown pools.

If he's taking me upstairs that means I'll see others. People who could possibly help me. Maybe just maybe, I can get out.

"You don't have a choice? Everybody has choices, Wolfe,"

I murmur his name, as if I'm savoring it. As if it's a delicacy. Something to be relished and appreciated. "Let me leave? You can turn a blind eye. I could run." It's the first time I mention this to him, and for a moment it looks as if he's going to agree, but then he shakes his head and my stomach plummets.

"Firebird, you're too feisty." He closes the distance between us, swallowing up the air, and I'm immediately breathless from his proximity. My lungs gasp for the air that's been stolen, but he's the only one who can give it back. Lifting my chin, I meet his gaze dead on.

"Then you should discipline me," I taunt him, hoping that my feisty mouth will make him see I can get out. I just need a chance. One strong hand reaches for my face, and I flinch, expecting a harsh slap, but what he does is something far worse. He lightly strokes his fingers over my cheek. My skin tingles, alight with electricity.

"Phoenix, don't taunt me, please," he pleads, dropping his gaze from me momentarily, and I immediately miss it. It's the first time he's called me Phoenix, the mythological firebird and it warms my heart in a way I've never felt.

"Why? You hurt me. You make me want you, come all over your tongue and fingers and then you leave. How do you think that feels?" My words add fuel to his already maddened expression, but I don't care. A fire deep in my gut blazes. "You listen to me for a change. I've never seen you. You've seen more of me than any man ever has, yet you expect me to just sit back quietly and agree to all your demands? To stop taunting you?" My mouth purses in a tight line, my arms cross in front of my chest. I wait a moment for him to respond, but he just stares at me.

I decide to up my game. If I can't reach him by talking, then I'll make him feel. Reaching for the sheer white dress I'm wearing, I pull hard, and the soft material rips open. I'm bare. His gaze trails from my eyes, down my body, so slowly it feels as if his hands are on me. Teasing me, stroking me, making me ache with need.

"Jesus, Phoenix," he bites out—growls even—but his gaze lingers. As if he needs to see me. He needs to feast on me with his eyes.

"What? Can't handle me? Am I too much for you?" That's when he breaks. Without warning, I'm dragged off the bed and shoved against the wall, my breasts squashed against the cold tiles.

"Do you want this?" he bites out, growling at me as he presses his thick erection against my ass. I can't move. My head is pressed against the solid surface. His lips whisper over my ear, and my body is aflame with an ache so feral and animalistic, so deep in my core, I swear it's in my soul. "Let me tell you something, Paige. I'm nice, to a certain extent. Don't get me wrong, I may be gentle with you, but I do enjoy hurting you too. When you cry out, when you scream, it makes my dick hard, and I want to shove it so far inside your body, it will feel as if I'm climbing inside not only your sweet, wet cunt, but into your mind. So, when you taunt me, it makes my blood boil, and I want to fuck you until you can't stand. When the only thing you'll want, or need between your thighs, is me. And as much as I can't have you forever, I fucking want it so much. I'm going to be sent to hell for it."

"Then take me to the fiery pit with you, Wolfe." He spins me around, keeping our bodies flush, but rigid with need. All he does is stare at me with a gaze so piercing, so damn consuming, it feels as if I'm about to combust. "Show me your face, let me see you."

He shakes his head, turning those dark eyes to the bed. "I can't. I don't want you to see the monster behind the mask." His words grip my heart, squeezing the air from my lungs, and tears prick my eyes. Reaching out, I touch the smooth material of the mask which sits flush against his face. "You shouldn't want me," he warns, but I'm not scared. I place a finger under his chin, forcing him to look at me.

"I'm not scared of you, Wolfe. I trust you," I confess, and I see the flames dance behind those chocolate pools.

"Jesus, Firebird, you can't, I..." He leans in, his lips inches from mine. The heat of his breath fans over my face, sending fire rushing through my veins.

"Just take me and make me yours. Then nobody will be able to touch me, right?" I know it's a lie. I'll still be used. But I want him to be my first. To claim me before any other man does. "Be my first. I'd rather have a man that I want to do it." His gaze lifts in shock, pinning me to the spot. I hold my breath, waiting for him to deny me, but he reaches for me and lifts me to wrap my legs around his waist.

"I could get into so much shit for this, Paige. For taking your innocence," he confesses, pain making his tone raspy, but I roll my hips and press my core against his erection.

"Please, Sir," I murmur the words he loves and his restraint snaps releasing the beast within. He holds on to my hips, and walks us over to the bed. Placing me on my feet, he steps back and narrows his gaze.

"Lie back," he orders—ever the Dominant—and I obey easily. Flutters in my belly taunt me, and I can't help the excitement that stirs deep inside me. Losing my virginity was never something I gave much thought to. I'd never given much thought to sex, but right now, with this man who's standing before me in his tight-fitting white dress shirt, a pair of black slacks, and a mask, I need him. I want him. "Open your legs. Get yourself wet for me," he orders.

My hand falls between my thighs, and I find I'm already wet. Slick with need. "I'm..." My words taper off, and I know I'm blushing. The heat on my cheeks is evidence that the embarrassment is clear.

"You're already needy for me, Firebird?" I nod and he smirks. "Good girl," he says with reverence. "This isn't going to be gentle. I don't know if I can hold back with you, Paige. You've..." He stops and his hands unbutton the shirt, letting it pool on the floor at his feet. His smooth skin is lightly tanned. Taut muscles greet me now that he's no longer hidden behind a hoodie.

When his slacks fall to his thick, muscled thighs, I gasp at the erection that juts out at me. I watch in awe as he rips the foil wrapper and sheaths himself. I open my mouth to say something. "I..."

"We don't have to—" he says, but I cut off his words.

"Yes, we do." I nod. "Fuck me, please," I beg in a breathy tone. My body is trembling on the bed as I lay spread before him. My fingers on the bundle of nerves. Without any more words passing between us, he settles over me, pressing me into the bed.

He nudges my opening with the tip of his cock and my body tingles. Electric currents shoot through me at an alarming pace as I grip his shoulders. His hips move and he enters me. "Fuck, that's tight," he groans, dropping his forehead to mine. Our eyes are locked. "This isn't going to be gentle."

"Do it."

Before I have time to think, he plunges fully into me and I cry out at being spread open so wide. "Oh god!" A searing pain shoots through me, and I bite down on his shoulder to keep from screaming.

"I'm sorry, baby. I'm so sorry," he murmurs reverently.

"It's okay, I'm okay." A small smile plays on my lips and he gifts me one back. My heart is in my throat. Tears burn my eyes, but they're not from the sharp pain, they're from all the emotion that seems to be stealing the breath from my lungs.

"You're so tight. So damn perfect," he grunts as his hips thrust back and forth into mine. Each time he stills allowing me time to adjust. "I can't—" Reaching for his ass, I grip him, pulling him into me. Needing the pain, wanting the ache to ease. And I know only he can do it.

"Don't stop," I hiss through my teeth as the pain and pleasure whirl together in an unending maelstrom, sending me into orbit. My legs tighten around his hips as he bucks against me. Slow at first, but when our eyes meet it's there. A living breathing entity between us as our bodies connect in the most primal way. Love. We don't say it. We don't need to. It's part of us.

His hips roll back and forth, slowly, torturously, but he obeys me for once and fucks me. He's not gentle, he's not sweet and loving, but it's the most incredible feeling. He isn't just fucking me. He's inhaling me, consuming me, and utterly owning me.

This man I covet is giving me everything I want and need, and as our bodies mold and soar, I dig my nails into the soft skin of his tight, muscled ass and hold him inside me. As if I'll shatter when he pulls out.

Our breathing is ragged. Needy. His body tenses as mine tightens. Everything below my belly button tugs with desire, and I know I'm about to have my first orgasm with a man inside me.

My body bows off the bed, and my eyes shut tight, but he

growls in my ear, "Look at me, Firebird. See who's taking you. Look at the man claiming you, fucking you." His words have me snapping my eyes open to meet his, and I crest, my body locks, and I shudder through an orgasm that steals not only my breath but my heart, and I know he's just seared my soul.

NINE

Kael

IT'S BEEN A WEEK SINCE I TOOK PAIGE. I SHOULDN'T HAVE taken her the way I did. I should have been gentle, loving, but when she begged, I couldn't hold back. I turned into the monster I always feared I would be. Since then, she hasn't left my mind, and I haven't been back to train her because I don't know if I can restrain myself.

Something happened when I fucked her innocence away. It hit me deep in the gut. My heart ached, but I knew it would, because she captured me the first time I laid my eyes on her. She crawled inside me, shattered the dark soul, burning it to ash. Against my father's wishes and rules, I've made things very personal with this girl, and she'll ruin me.

Stalking down the hallway, my sister Theia comes bounding up to me in her usual cheerful way. "Kael, have you seen Sam? I wanted to say goodbye. I'm heading out today, and I guess I should see him before I go."

"No, I think he's at the warehouse."

She pouts. "He's avoiding me."

"Is it because of Dax? Did he find out about you two?" My sister, who plays the innocent with my father, has been fucking our head of security for about a year now. She's twenty-one and he's thirty-four. As much as I hate their relationship, I've never seen my sister happier, and I know Dax is a good man. There's something about him I trust. If my sister had to be with any one of the assholes in here, I'd prefer for it to be him.

"No, well, I don't know. I think Sammy saw us in one of the rooms the other day," she confesses, biting her lip and peering up at me under dark lashes.

"Jesus, Theia, you need to be careful."

"I can't help it if he's got cameras in the rooms," she retorts petulantly, and I can't help chuckling. I'm sure my brother is scarred for life, seeing his little sister bound and whipped.

"Is he good to you? Do you love him?" I stare at her, and she nods. I know she wouldn't lie to me. And if Dax ever hurts her, I'll fucking kill him. "You tell me if he ever does wrong by you, okay?"

"Yes, Kael. You know I will." She reaches up on tiptoes to kiss me on the cheek before disappearing down the long hallway, leaving me to face my firebird alone.

I left a note under her door, which I hope she found. It had an order for her to wear something I've been dying to see her in, and I hope she obeys.

As the door swings open, I find her on the floor. She's

kneeling in her presentation pose, her head lowered and her eyes focused on the carpet before her. Delicate hands on each thigh, flat, palms down. Flowing red hair cascades down her back like flames licking at her body, attempting to consume her. That's my job. My ache and need. I covet this girl more than I want to admit. More than I should.

She's perfect. In every way.

The black corset that hugs her curves shimmers. Seeing her kneel for me tugs at my restraint not to fuck her senseless, but it also fills me with pride that she's mine. I ache with a pain so deep in my gut to take her again, to make her scream and beg for me not to stop, but to fuck her harder. There's something beautiful about a woman begging for savagery.

"Eyes up. Sit on your heels and place your hands behind your back." She obeys, straightening her spine, which in turn juts her breasts out of the low-cut material. Her rose-colored nipples are hard peaks, ready for my mouth, and my clamps. She twines her hands behind her, and meets my gaze with fire dancing in those emerald pools. "Good girl," I growl and she purrs, just like I knew she would.

"Are we training today?" she asks with a small smile, and I nod.

Perhaps I can talk to Dax about helping me break Paige out of here. He's always said he'd do anything for me, my sister, and Sam, but to ask him to go against my father not only puts him in danger, but everyone involved as well.

"We are. Today will be difficult for you because you'll get a taste of what is expected of you when you reach those doors," I inform her, knowing it's going to not only hurt her, but rip me apart to have to whip her until I draw blood. I've been gentle and caring, but today I need to be the brutal thug, just like those who come in here to live out their sickest fantasies.

"I know they'll hurt me. I've seen the scars on Scarlett when she's come to bring in my breakfast." Her confident words gut me. I don't want her to hurt.

"This place is dangerous. Don't get tangled up in friendships. Don't show affection or emotion." My words are the truth, but deep down I know I'm a hypocrite, because I've already done everything I just warned her against.

"Is that what you're doing here? Not showing emotion?" Her words ring true, so true that they scare me. Glancing at her, I crook my finger, summoning her closer. She rises gracefully, padding over to me.

"We're going to the training room. Hand me your leash." She obeys by lifting the leather strap, which in turn clinks the chain attached to her collar. Her obedience lights up her face, and when she glances at me, I don't admonish her because when her eyes meet mine, I want them there. I can't bring myself to not have her look at me. Because, in her anger, in her fear, and trepidation I see it, so clearly it guts me.

She's falling. If only she knew I'd fallen a long time ago. The first time I laid my eyes on her. I tug her leash and she follows on her knees. Once we get to the hallway, all I want to do is tell her to walk beside me, but my father is in the mansion today, so I need to play it safe and let her crawl two steps behind me.

"Kael." *Speak of the devil.* Glancing up, I find my father dressed in a dark pair of slacks and a black shirt. He's not masked, which is a new development, but I don't say anything.

Instead, I nod in greeting, "Father." The hate I have for this man isn't unfounded. It's not a secret either. He crouches, reaching for Paige, and my body goes rigid with tension. He's brutal, he's ruthless, and he takes no prisoners when it comes to the submissives.

"Father?!" Paige's voice is incredulous, and I cringe at her knowing I'm Harlan's son. Tugging the leash, I pin her with a warning glare.

He grips her long, flowing, red hair and tugs her head back. "How is this little one doing?" he asks, his cold stare pinned on Paige. The way he looks at her makes me sick. It's a hungry desire, dark and sinful. Something in his eyes tells me he wants her.

"Don't touch me!" she spits in his face, and he chuckles darkly. Her fire is beautiful, but he'll hurt her. I pull on her leash, bringing her face to mine.

"Shut. Up." My hiss is filled with venom, and all I can do is hope she obeys me this time. The tension that seeps through my veins burns, reinforcing my need to protect her.

Mine.

The word is unbidden. One glance at the predatory gaze on my father's face tells me that he covets her as much as I do, because she's not ours. She's here to work, to please the clients. Not us. But that's never stopped my father before.

"Fuck you both!" *Jesus, this woman.* Without thinking, I drag her down the hallway.

"As you can see, Father, I have work to do." I steel my gaze when he glances up. My father is someone not to be deceived. It is an impossible feat to accomplish. Because he's a master at picking the pieces of the soul from just a mere glance into someone's eyes. Knowing a person's innermost desires and using them against them.

"She does need a lot of work," he agrees with an evil glint in his eyes, his gaze roaming all over her entire body. Once, and then again. "I want to see you after you're done. There's something important I'd like to discuss"—he drops his eyes to my girl, to Paige, and reaches down, taking her chin in his hand and forcefully pulling her face up to meet his—"and you, little one, better behave. I'd love a taste of your sweet flesh before you turn twenty. So young, so beautiful. Redheads are supposed to be delicious." He chuckles. Rising to full height, he gives me one last glance and stalks down the corridor.

Releasing a breath I didn't realize I was holding, I cast a quick glance at Paige, only to find her looking up at me with curiosity and confusion. Tugging her leash, we head into the room and once the door is shut, I close my eyes, trying to calm myself.

"You're afraid of him," she states.

"If you don't shut your mouth, I'm going to make sure you don't forget you're here to be a fuck toy, not a goddamn opinionated woman!" I bite out angrily, so harsh I hear her gasp in shock at my outburst. With her little display out there we could have both been reprimanded.

A second later, I feel it. Warm hands on my shoulders. I realize she stood up, and her body is cocooned against mine. Like a kitten nestling in someone's arms, she's contentedly holding on to me as if I'm her lifeline. Only, as much as I know we're tethered to one another right now, something will snap the line, and I won't be able to keep her safe.

"On your knees!" I growl and she immediately drops. Obeying me like she's meant to, she keeps her eyes on the floor. "We can't... You can't..."

"But what if we found a way?" Her question is valid. We could possibly find a way.

"Paige. Stop. Just fucking stop." I turn to regard her, leaning in close to her face. Glistening emeralds pierce my soul. They practically rip my heart from its chest because I want her to see me. My face. To see the man who is breaking every damn rule for her. But I can't. So I take a deep breath and shut down. "Kneel on the sofa, grip the back and hold on. This time there will be no gentle spanks, there will be no soothing. Today I'm going to hurt you. I'm going to make you cry. And I'm going to make you bleed."

Her gasp fans over the half of my face that isn't covered. The clean-shaven flesh is warm with her sweet breath. "But—"

"Now." The stern tone of my voice is evident. She doesn't say anything else. Instead, she pads over to the sofa in question and settles on her knees, her hands on the smooth leather and her body trembling. She's scared. I've never hurt her before. Over the last month I've been gentle, but today, I need to be someone else. This time I'm going to take on the confidence of a man I've looked up to all my life. One that I refused to mimic, but I know I must. If she's ever to survive this, she'll need to experience me unleashed.

Today, I'll be like my brother.

But I'll be a better version. Because once I make her cry, after I make her bleed, I'll soothe her so she knows who she truly belongs to.

Picking up the leather belt I've been avoiding, I unravel it while I step up behind her. "Pull your panties down. I want to see your creamy ass," I order. She pushes her panties down to her thighs and I'm met with her bare flesh. So beautiful. My breathing comes out ragged and labored at the effect she's having on me. "Keep your back arched. I'm going to mark you. I want you to count each swat, no screaming. Be a good girl." She nods. "Words, Firebird."

"Yes, Sir."

Jesus, every time she says that, I want to save her. I want to claim her. Make her mine. Lifting the belt, I bring it down with a soft swish through the air. The crack is loud as it hits her skin. A whimper. A barely audible sound falls from her lips, but she doesn't scream. She obeys.

"One." Her voice is strong, but I can hear the agony dripping from that one word.

Shutting my eyes, I allow my frustration to take over.

Without warning, I release a second swat. "Two."

And another.

"Three."

The reddened skin is luminous. Welts rise on her smooth, porcelain skin.

"Four."

With each lash, she counts and my throat closes, but I continue.

"Five." The marks on her pale skin are bright and angry. "Six." My body trembles, shaking with agony, not physical, but emotional. "Seven." Her voice breaks. Tears are streaming down her face. I can see them glisten from my viewpoint as they leak from her pretty eyes. "Eight."

The buckle bites into my hand, but it's the globes of her

ass that break and I notice the blood trickling from the lashes. Crimson agony taunts me. Confirming what I am. A monster.

"Nine." She continues. Her fire still burns. I need her to break for me. To give me the one thing I know she'll never gift anyone. My teeth grind in anger, and I see red. Nothing else. I see violence. I see agony. I see the woman I want to love devastated before me. "Ten." That tenth one cuts into the already reddened skin. My lungs give out. My heart breaks through my chest. A thick lump forms in my throat.

Emotion so profound chokes me, and I know I can't continue. Dropping my hand, I watch her body shake. I know she's trying to be quiet after I've obliterated all the trust we've built around us. The walls that shielded us have crumbled. And so have we.

Her ass is bright red. A beautiful color, and I want to kneel behind her and soothe her. Before I can say anything, she shocks me when she turns, her gaze meeting mine, and she offers me a watery smile. "Do it. I can take it, for you." Then she faces forward and arches her back so beautifully, so fucking perfectly, all I want to do is fuck her.

I'm panting now. "Spread your legs." My order is clear in the silence of the room. Her thighs open, showing me her pussy. Her glistening, slick sex. "You're wet." My tone is filled with astonishment.

"Yes, Sir," she breathes. My hand opens, and the belt falls to the ground with a loud clang, which echoes around us. It's a warning. *Don't get personal.* But I no longer adhere to it. Pulling my shirt from the waistband of my slacks, I drop it to the floor. Her body is inviting, enticing, calling to me like a siren's song. Shoving my dress pants down my legs, I step out of my shoes, and I'm left in nothing but a pair of boxer briefs and sporting a thick erection.

"I want you, Paige. I want every inch of you. To claim you." Lifting my hands, I gently place them on her reddened cheeks and massage them. Her moans and whimpers fuel me to continue my ministrations. "Is this what you want? To be my submissive?" She nods, and I know it's what she wants, but I need her words. I want to hear her voice those words gifting me her submission. "Tell me, please."

"I want you, my Wolfe. I'm yours. I've been yours. Don't you see it?" I do. But I don't tell her. Instead, I push my briefs to my thighs. Gripping my steel shaft, I tease it along her lips. We moan in unison at the contact. She's drenched, and I slowly push into her. Entering her body is like coming home. It's as if I've been wandering the world with no sustenance, but as soon as I'm connected to her, I've found my purpose. My value.

"Paige, I can't hold back." It's the second time I've been inside her, but this time, there are no barriers. Skin on skin. Heat against heat. And I'm a man lost in oblivion. In heaven. In the most euphoric emotion, which I should have never let myself dive into. But it's too late. We're past the point of no return.

"I love you, Wolfe." Her words echo the ones in my head, and my gaze snaps open.

"What?" I grunt, as I fully seat myself inside her body.

"I love you." Without responding, I grip her hips and pull out to the tip before slamming back in. Deep and fast, stealing the breath from her lungs because it belongs to me. Again and again. I fuck her. Mercilessly.

I'm brutal with hunger.

I'm violent with need.

I'm rough with desire.

Her body tenses, pulsing around me. "I'm going to—"

"Wait, hold it," I bite out through clenched teeth. I want us together. Another two thrusts. I reach around her, pinching her clit. "Now." And she unravels. She flies, then soars for me.

Like a firebird.

Like the Phoenix.

And it's in that moment when I tell her.

"I love you too, Paige."

MY WARMTH, YOUR FUEL

Like a flame in the darkness,
Your presence gives me warmth,
Mine gives you fuel and
Together we burn

TEN

Paige

MY DOOR FLYING OPEN STARTLES ME FROM A DREAMLESS sleep. "Get up." A man I recognize stalks in, a man who isn't my Wolfe. His face is chiseled, like a statue made of the finest porcelain. He's handsome, but the expression he wears is severe. As if he's heard the worst news imaginable. The familiar cobalt eyes he pins me with are cold, aloof almost. He rounds my bed when I don't obey him and pulls me from the warmth. "This is your fault," he says, leaning in to my personal space. "As much as I want to be angry with you, though, I can't. You did him a favor," he hisses under his breath, and my confusion swirls with the fogginess from sleep.

"What?"

"He's gone, Paige. Today, you get me." His words ring in my mind like an alarm, screaming at me to wake up. *He's gone.* When I move, I still feel the sting on my ass. But it's the delicious agony between my legs that makes my emotions skyrocket. Only last night we confessed our love for each other. How can he leave after telling me that?

"I don't... I mean... Why?"

"Get dressed. Don't ask too many questions and you'll probably get out of here alive. I'll be back in fifteen minutes. You best be ready for me." That's all he says before leaving me to get ready for the day.

My once beating heart stills. It's a pain like I've never known before.

I gave him everything.

My life.

My body.

I even offered him my heart and soul and he just walked out.

It doesn't make sense. He told me he loves me.

I'm young, but I'm not naïve. Or perhaps I am. I believed a man who enjoyed hurting me. I'd fallen in love with my captor. With someone who I'd never even seen. The month I've spent with him has allowed me to change considerably. I've grown from a scared eighteen-year-old virgin, into a woman who wants, aches, and desires.

Pushing off the bed, I pad over to my bathroom and open the door. It's still dark as I step inside. Once I've freshened up and made my way back to my bedroom, I find Samael, the man I first met on my eighteenth birthday with the cold blue eyes sitting on my dresser. It's such a youthful thing to do that I can't help frowning at him.

"Paige, we need to talk. I need you to listen to me very carefully," he says, his tone serious. But where his stern glare met mine before, it has now been replaced with a softened stare.

"I don't know why—"

"He had to go. He didn't have a choice. I can't tell you any more than that, but there's a bigger problem you need to worry about than him." He pushes off the dresser and heads toward me. When he reaches me, he lifts my chin with his index finger and looks at me. He pierces me with blue pools of curiosity. "You loved him." It's a statement, but I nod in response. He lifts his chin. "Well, it's time to be strong because that emotion will be your downfall, Paige."

"But—"

"You've been summoned by the one man who will most definitely break you, the owner of this fine establishment. He believes you're the reason for all this trouble. You best be strong. I hope Wolfe trained you to take pain." At the mention of his name, the hole in my chest only gapes wider, leaving me a heaving mess. Strong arms drag me to the bed and settle me on the soft mattress.

"I-I... How—"

"Look at me," Sam's commanding tone has me snapping my gaze to his. "It is your fault he's gone. He's the only one who could have saved you and he's been sent away. Don't ask fucking questions. Do not let your guard down. This isn't easy. You'll learn that. You'll cry and hurt. There will be days where the pain will be too much. And you know what? I'll be the one to dole out that agony on your sweet, supple body. Your heart may be shattered to pieces, but your body soon will hurt worse than any heartbreak."

His words shatter me more than I thought they could. I've lost Wolfe, and now I'm stuck here in this hell without the man I love. I meet Sam's gaze, attempting to steel myself against the agony that's slowly burning its way through me.

Inhaling a deep breath, I straighten my shoulders and nod. I dig deep and in the depths of my soul that only *he* touched, I find strength. "I'm strong enough to endure anything you throw at me," I bite out as anger slowly fuels me. It's then that I'm awarded a smile. I've never seen this man with anything other than a look of fierce danger on his face, but as he smiles, there's so much more to the trainer they call the Grim Reaper. "Do I call you Sam or Samael?"

"You can call me Sam," he affirms, but doesn't give anything more away.

"Sam, I like it." I offer a smile without happiness.

"You shouldn't. You should fear me, little one." He traces his finger over my lower lip, deep blue orbs following the movement in a heated gaze. "I would much rather you call me, Sir, but there's only one who owns you and it isn't me." The memory of the man who does own me flashes through my mind, and a gasp falls from my lips. "Delicious," he murmurs on a sinful smirk. His eyes bore a hole into my lip as he regards it in awe. "You tasted so good that night, I almost claimed you as my own."

His words instill confidence in me. Somehow this man who I'm meant to fear allows me to draw strength from him. "Take me to my fate. I'm ready," I declare. Squaring my shoulders, I meet his gaze and he nods.

"Good girl."

"Hello, Paige." The gruff tone of a masked man who I recognize is Harlan Wolfe, comes from the depths of the darkened room. Although, the rasp of his voice is slightly different to what I remember when I first met him, there's a distinct way he says my name that has revulsion skittering through me.

Sam brought me in here. The room itself is cold, making goosebumps dot my skin. There's a dim light bulb hanging from the high ceiling which sets the room in an eerie glow. He gave me explicit instructions—do not speak or beg, and obey orders. The tension that radiated through him was palpable, adding to the fear of what I'm about to encounter. It's so dark, I can just about make out that there are four walls, a small window high above me, and a door to my left.

My hands and feet are bound to a wooden *X* shape, which

makes me wonder if I'm being sacrificed for falling in love with the man who trained me.

"I've heard some wonderful things about your sweet body." He says as he nears me and I can fully make out the smirk that I saw in the hallway. "I'm here to teach you a lesson. To show you that little sluts like you are made for only one thing. You see, my family has been running this business for a long time," he says this with pride lacing his tone. Proud of the vile things he does. "And not you or any one of you other whores are going to destroy that."

He stalks toward me and reaches for something on the table. A flick of a lighter echoes through the space then the flame of a candle lights up the room.

It reminds me of a cellar, or basement. My body shivers as his dark eyes trail from my toes up my bare legs and over my panty-clad sex. He stops momentarily on my flat stomach and then lifts his eyes to my breasts, which are thankfully covered by my bra. But I might as well be naked from the hunger that dances in his eyes, which are lit up by the flickering flame.

A sound startles me from the corner, and I see another masked figure sitting in a chair. He's far from me so I can't see his face, but I notice his hand move to his crotch, which makes me want to retch. Tears burn my eyes. Two men. I've only ever been with my Wolfe.

"She's a pretty bird," the stranger grunts from his voyeuristic corner. I allow my mind to flit through the partners my father worked with, but I don't recognize his voice. I wonder who he could be. He rises then, taking two steps toward me and I notice he is older, his voice along with the gray hair gives me an indication that he may be close to Harlan's age. To my father's age.

I want to beg for my life, for them to let me go, but Sam told me not to talk, not to beg, not to say anything. All I need to do is endure. Even though my pain and anger fuel me, I'm going to trust him and do what I need to, to get through this.

"Now," Harlan says while reaching for something from beside me. When he straightens, I notice he's holding a blade. "You're going to learn what your body should be used for." With that, he slices the material covering the most intimate parts of my body, and I'm left splayed open to his filthy leer. The second man stalks closer. Dressed in an immaculate charcoal suit, and a crisp white dress shirt, he looks like he should be seated in a boardroom, not here in this depraved dungeon. He doesn't speak again. He merely observes.

They both take in my bare skin, and fear sends ice racing through my veins.

There was only one man who ever saw me naked.

The one I gave my heart to.

"What a pretty cunt." His cold eyes drink me in like I'm the most decadent thing he's ever seen. "We're going to fuck it so hard. We'll break you, little red."

He lifts a finger and trails it over my breasts, slow and meticulous. His touch is ice, his smirk is vile, and the way he leans in and runs his nose along my jaw is poison. I shut my eyes and go back, all the way back to Wolfe. The man who took my virginity, along with my heart and soul.

"When we're done, you'll forget all about the illusion of love. You'll realize that emotions like that are not for temptresses like you. You're a toy. You're a pet for men like us to enjoy. You're the payment for services rendered. Now, the debt needs to be settled. Oh, and let me tell you something," he says, leaning in farther. His hot breath fans over my face, which has bile rising in my throat. "When you cry, when you scream, when you beg for me to stop, we'll only do it harder and deeper. We'll fuck you raw. Until you're bleeding on our cocks."

His fingers reach my core and before I have time to blink, he plunges them deep inside me. I'm dry, it burns, and the sting is worse than any lashing I've ever felt. He pumps his fingers in and out, again and again. A plea sits on the tip of my tongue, begging to be let loose, but I refrain, I stay strong.

Another pair of hands grab my breasts. Fingers tug my nipples, pulling them until I can't be silent, and I cry out. I scream so loud, my throat burns. The agony between my legs, the intense pain that shoots through my nipples, has me wanting to close my eyes and drift into the afterlife.

Suddenly, the finger is pulled from my core, and he grunts in my face. "Look at me you slut." A harsh grip on my chin has me facing him. "I want you to cry, I want you to beg." Smirking and lifting his fingers to his mouth, he sucks on them while staring at me dead on. My body convulses as I retch.

Thick fingers and a firm grip take hold of my neck, squeezing until I see stars. My breathing is ragged and my lungs scream for air. My arms tug in their restraints and tears spring to my eyes. "P-p-p..." Words fail me and Harlan's sneer is evident even in the mask.

"So pretty when you're about to die. But, I don't like dead toys, I want them to fight me. I like making sure they feel exactly what it's like to hurt." Suddenly, he releases my throat and my gasps echo in the room. *Where is he? Why doesn't he save me?* The questions race through my mind, but it's no use. Because I have my answer. He left. I'm here alone. I must survive.

And that's when Sam's words filter through my agony.

Be strong, Firebird. He's gone, but I'm here.

The blade my tormentor used to slice away my clothes shimmers in the dim light of the candle as he weaves it over the open flame. He turns to me with the hot blade, and my heart leaps into my throat. *Oh, God! No!* The searing pain of hot metal on flesh is something I wouldn't wish on my worst enemy. My body shudders, and the bile I tried expelling earlier rises until I puke. It feels as if my guts have been ripped from my throat.

"Look how pretty your skin looks," he grunts with reverence. Another few minutes that feel like an eternity over the flame. He brings the red-hot knife to my bare stomach and traces a *W* just below my ribs. "That's because you're a whore, Paige Madden. That's all you'll ever be. All you're made for," he hisses, and the tears I've tried to keep at bay topple and stream down my cheeks like rivers of pain attempting to rid me of the agony.

Only, I'll never be cured.

Salvation is something I'll never know.

My screams echo in the cavernous room.

He drops the knife with a loud clang on the table. When my eyes open, I notice the blood seeping from the open wound. I watch in horror when Harlan lifts a silver hook. "Untie her and turn her around, we're going to play."

The stranger obeys. Once I'm free, he grips my hair, pulling me over to a dark wooden table in the center of the room. "Kneel," he grunts. Once I'm on the flat surface, he proceeds in tying my wrists to my ankles, leaving my legs spread obscenely. I'm completely incapacitated.

When the cold metal trails over my ass, I can't stop the shudder that races through me. The sharp tip is at my virgin, puckered hole, seeking entrance. I'm tense, it's going to hurt, and it does. He pushes it in, slowly, but he's not gentle. The agony at being ripped open—the steel is like ice entering me.

Once it's inside me, one of the men, I can't see who attaches a rope to the collar around my neck. "If you move, you'll rip this pretty ass open. Best you stay still, pet." The tether is taut, and even the slightest movement warns me that he's right.

My tears flow freely, incoherent words fall from my lips. Then I hear it. A belt buckle. A foil wrapper. And I pray. But no God can save me now. A thick erection is slammed into my pussy, the pain is excruciating and I beg and plead. I break. In that moment, nothing can stop me shattering. The old man grunts as he fucks me. I'm tugged up by my hair and another cock is shoved down my throat.

I'm not used to it and the urge to puke is at the forefront of my mind. Pain. So much agony, I can't breathe. The man in my mouth holds my head down, my nose touching the pubic hair at his crotch as I choke on his shaft.

"That's it, pet. Choke on it. If you puke I'll make you lick it up, filthy bitch." He grunts, slamming into my throat again and again. There's no reprieve. The hook in my ass tugs as both men violate me in a way I don't think I'll ever return from.

My mind shuts down. It's vacant because I go to a place where I'm safe. Where he's there and I'm in his arms.

And as I'm taken by force, I allow myself to drift to nothing.

To the dark.

ELEVEN

Kael

THE DARK SKY HAS THE OMINOUS FEELING IN MY GUT churning. She's going to be taken, broken and I know there's nothing I can do. I was forced out of the house, leaving her to fend for herself. I have nothing. Flopping onto the bed, I stare at the ceiling and picture her. Long, flowing red hair, emerald green eyes. Sweet, sensual curves. Her creamy skin that turned rosy with my handprint. All that pulled me in. But what kept me enthralled was her smile. When she gifted me one, it was as if my world had lit up for the first time in years. She became my focus, and I lost her.

The sounds of sex filter down to the bedroom where I'm currently lying. My best friend, Axel, is a man whore, but he's given me a place to stay. I can't complain. But it's the fact that he's fucking his way through the city, while my heart lies back in Caged, which has me second-guessing my choice of accommodation.

Closing my eyes, I recall the memory of my father disowning

me. It doesn't matter if he doesn't consider me a Wolfe any longer. The only thing of value that I had in my life was my Phoenix.

"Sit." *My father glares at me, and dread fills my veins as it riddles my body with a shudder. The chair I settle in is uncomfortable, not because of the actual seat, instead it's the prickling awareness that my father must have found out. He stands behind his desk, hands in his pant pockets, feigning a casual demeanor I know well he does not possess. Lifting my eyes, I meet his blue ones, they're cold, icy and feral.* "I've come to notice a few things about you, son." *He settles in his leather chair opposite me. There's a barely controlled rage that drips from his words.*

"I'm not sure—"

"Oh, Kael. Don't lie to me. I can read you a mile away, you know." *He smirks. His fingers steeple in front of his mouth as he regards me.* "You and Sam have always been different. At first, I thought it was a good thing. But, now I feel differently. It has been brought to my attention you've let your feelings get in the way of your work."

"No, I'd never do that."

"Kael, should I mention the redhead?" *His question jars me, and I sit back, my mouth pursed in a thin line. Shit. How could he know?* "She's certainly beautiful. She'll be an attraction for many clients. And as much as I'm interested in seeing her starting in the rooms soon I'd like to get her on the floor. Tonight. Do you think she's ready?"

"Not yet," *I respond, hoping he doesn't notice the tick in my jaw.*

His glance on me doesn't linger as he nods slowly. "Funny you should say that, I think she is. I want her on the floor tonight. In fact, I've got two clients who would love to see her curves." *Fisting my hands* was a mistake because his gaze drops and narrows in on them, then lifts to my face. The emotion must be written all over it because as soon as our eyes lock it's done.

"Father—"

"These are your papers." He shoves an envelope toward me. "They'll explain exactly what happens now that you've been disowned. You're also to pack a bag, one bag, and depart immediately. Dax will escort you off the property safely. You should have known better. These are mere whores."

"She's not—"

"Exactly! I want you out of this house, off my property immediately. You thought I wouldn't notice the sweet, loving touches. The soft, soothing words?" He rises, rounding the desk, and stalks toward me. "You knew the rules. No personal attachments. They only end in fucking disaster. Your mother learned that when your sister killed her by being born. Women are nothing. They're toys to be used. I want you out. You're no son of mine."

I push off the chair and stalk toward him. "If I'm leaving, she is too. I want her. You can keep all my belongings. Just give me Paige." The words have barely left my mouth before the sting of his punch leaves me tasting metal. The gold ring my father always wears on his left hand bites into my lip, leaving crimson dripping from my mouth.

"She stays. You're out."

"I'm not leaving without her."

"We'll see about that." He crooks his finger, and I realize we're no longer alone. Along with Dax are two men who look like they could possibly break me in half with a snap of their fingers. "Kael needs to be escorted off the property, immediately." Without another glance at me, the man who I called father turns his back on me.

"Father, listen to me, I'm not—"

He pivots, pinning me with a glower of disapproval. "If you don't leave quietly, I'll bring her in here right now and show you how a whore is meant to be treated. Do you want to watch while I fuck her holes? Because I will." His words send revulsion coursing through my veins. Knowing I have no choice, I turn and stalk out, meeting Dax's eyes, seeing the apology that flashes in them. Two guards grip my arms and tug me along. I can't help fighting them off, but my father bellows an order. "Teach him a lesson while you're at it. Then take him to the gate. He leaves with nothing."

That's all these thugs need to hear before they shove me down and land one kick to the ribs, another to the face. The pain that shoots through me is no worse than the thought of what's going to happen to Paige. Fists fly, connecting with my face and jaw.

Groaning in agony, I roll over, trying to shield myself. But it's no use, two of them, one of me. I deserve it. I hurt her and now I'm paying the price.

"That's enough, let's go," Dax's cool tone halts their movements. Even though my father is in charge, they will listen to the man who's head of security. Dax tugs me up and half drags me toward the exit. When I step outside, I leave my soul in the house. In the room where she lies waiting for me.

As we reach the gates I find Samael waiting on me. "I told you to be careful brother," he says. The confident smirk I've come to recognize on my brother's face is noticeably lacking as he takes in the blood dripping from my face. "You look like shit."

"You knew he was going to do this?" He shakes his head. Is that *sadness on his face?*

"Look, Kael. You may hate me, and that's okay, but I never wanted this to happen." For the first time in a long while I see sincerity in those blue eyes. "I know you love her," he states matter-of-factly. I don't respond, merely a nod tells him he's right.

"I need your help. Sneak me back in. I can get her, we can both leave and we'll be free. Samael, please?" I turn to my brother then. Meeting his gaze, I implore him.

"You know he'll not think twice about killing you. Or her for that matter. I can't see that happen, brother. Trust me when I say, I'll be there for her." We stare at each other, the hatred and anger we've become accustomed to fades and I see him for the first time. I see my brother.

"I'll come back for her." I vow. But I know he's right, I can't go back in there now. "Please look after her?" I sound like a goddamn woman.

Cobalt eyes stare through me, seeing my soul. It's then that he recognizes it and utters. "You're really in love with her." I can't voice my agreement, so I nod. "We'll both look after her," my brother gestures to the other man who's waiting behind me. When I turn to Dax, he affirms with a nod.

"I'm sorry, Kael, he called me in suddenly. I didn't know what was happening until I overheard what he said to you." I know he's not lying, because his eyes speak with more honesty than any words could. "I'll get her out of here. Somehow."

"We will." Turning to Sam, I see a hint of the human side of him and all I can do is hope.

Anger runs rife through me, and I can't help but land my fist in the wall beside the bed. Blood seeps from my knuckles, but I savor the ache. The pain.

It was my fault for allowing myself to feel. To finally believe that happiness wasn't merely what other people had. The thoughts of her, of what she's going to be put through, are worse than any ache or pain.

The only thing I can hope is for Sam to make sure she's strong. That she survives whatever they're going to throw at her. If my brother takes over as her trainer, I know she'll get through it. He's brutal. But I know my Firebird. If she has something other than a broken heart to focus on, she'll be okay.

I knew I couldn't give her a forever.

Deep down, every day I walked into her room, I knew something was going to obliterate us. And now as I lie alone with nothing but the thoughts racing through my mind on how to get back to the house to save her, I wonder what she's going through. If they've already hurt her. Just that thought alone makes me want to walk into that shithole and kill every last one of them.

She needs to be strong. She needs to fight because I'm going to fight for her. Somehow, I'll find a way to get back to her. Even if it's the last thing I do.

She never even saw my face. All those times we spent together, I didn't have the courage to show her the real me. I need to find a way to get her out. There must be something I can do to save her from what I know she's about to endure. Even though

I was the one who trained her, those monsters who frequent the club are not me. They'll hurt her beyond repair. What I fear most is that they'll not only break her body, but they'll shatter her mind.

I watch the sun rise from the window. Most of the night was spent formulating a plan. But each one I came up with left me or her dead which is not an option. I have no way of contacting her. No way of even speaking to her. I tried calling Sam, but he said my father has put the house on lock down. Cameras are now running twenty-four-seven in every room.

Pushing off the bed, I open the bedroom door to the sound of silence. I make my way into the kitchen to find a pot of coffee brewing. Axel must be up already. Perhaps he threw out whichever girl he'd been fucking the night before.

"Hey man," his voice comes from behind me as I fill a mug.

Dragging my gaze up, I meet Axe's cocky smirk. "Hey." He's dressed in a pair of jeans and a black Guns N Roses T-shirt.

"Sleep okay?" he asks, sauntering into the kitchen, grabbing his own mug and filling it with the freshly brewed coffee.

"Not really. Between you banging that chick and my mind racing a million miles a minute trying to figure out how to get my girl out of that place..." I let my words taper off when he turns to me.

"You need to clear your head. I'm leaving tonight, heading to New York. Come with me?" I glance at my best friend, who regards me with a narrowed blue stare. "Dax wants me back at Inferno while he's here at Caged. Somehow, I don't think I can let you out in the world by yourself. You look like shit, man." He sips his coffee as he regards me, and I know he's right. I'm a mess. Not only because of the black eye, bruises, and possible fractured ribs, but because I have no way of ever getting back into that house.

The need to get as far away from Caged as possible is running rife through my veins. "Then let's get this show on the road," I smirk, schooling my features so my best friend doesn't see the agony that's slowly seeping through my veins like a poison.

"Whoever she was, she's not worth it, man." He slaps my shoulder. Without responding, I turn and head back to the bedroom where I spent the night and start planning. Grabbing my phone, I hit dial on Dax's number. As soon as he answers, I ask the one question that's been on the tip of my tongue all night. "How is she?"

"I haven't seen her. Sam's been in there a couple of times. He told me your father called for her. I don't know what happened, but she is in her room. Sam said she's pretty broken."

"Dax, I need you to get her out of there. Or get me the fuck in there and I'll walk out with her. I'll burn the whole place down." My voice is urgent, the anger at my father using her, breaking her, is about to consume me.

"Kael, I need you levelheaded. I'm working with Sam. We'll get her out. Just trust me. If you come back here, you'll only make him angry. He will kill her. Then he'll kill you." He's right. I'm not thinking clearly.

"Get her out. Just save her. That's all that matters to me."

"I know." With that he hangs up, leaving me cursing the ground my father walks on. Dax's promise to get her out only gives me a moment's reprieve.

I can run, I can go to New York, but I know I'll never be able to leave her behind. There'll never be redemption for what I did to her. No salvation for what I left her to endure.

Rearing my hand back, I fling the phone against the wall, watching it shatter. Exactly like the love I hold for a woman who's probably going to be a shell when they're done with her. "Hey man, Dax just messaged to let me know he's got us a place to stay until we get ourselves sorted. Do you want to help me in the club? Security detail? Or..."

"No. I'm not cut out for that. I'll find my way. But I'll take you up on the offer of a place to stay until I find my own apartment."

He nods, closing the door again, and I pack up my meager belongings that Sam managed to salvage last night before I was thrown out. The drive into the city won't be long, and we'll get there by lunch time if we leave early enough.

As I stuff my clothes into the suitcase, I know it's time to trust in my brother. It will be a first. I just hope he doesn't let me down.

Now all that awaits me is a city that can swallow me whole. Perhaps a new life. But I know I'll never be able to rid myself of the memories. Those are ingrained in me, and there won't be any absolution from them.

In fact, I welcome them.

They remind me of something I'll never allow myself to do again.

Love.

EMPTINESS & LOVE

Your absence is my downfall
I reach for strength in our memories
Within my soul, I find us
I find you, I find me

TWELVE

Paige

Sam leads me up to the club. Tonight is the first time I'm scheduled to dance, and I'm nervous. I'm scared of what's going to happen if I mess up. "All you do is close yourself off. Just listen to the music, don't let anything they say get to you," he hisses beneath his breath.

"Yes, Sam." My voice is laden with fear. As soon as we step into the vast open space I'm jolted with shock. It's not a seedy, run down club like I had envisioned. It's elegant, dark colors accentuated by metal and glass. The dim lighting makes it seem less scary.

"That's your podium." Sam points at the small round stage in the one corner of the club which is surrounded by about ten tables all filled with men in black masks.

"Do I just dance?" I glance up, and for the first time in over a month I feel like that innocent eighteen year old girl who woke up in a strange bed, not a woman who fell in love with her captor.

Sam nods before escorting me to the stage, his fingers

lingering on my lower back almost protectively, and I want to hide in his arms. "Good luck, I'll be here," he murmurs in my ear before leaving me at the steps that lead up to the platform.

Tentatively, I make my way into the limelight and the men cheer and whistle causing my heart to deafen me with its thud in my ears. A song starts, "Skin" by Rihanna, and I shut my eyes, ignoring the voices. Picturing Wolfe, I move slowly at first. My knees are wobbly and I know I must find my strength somewhere.

Rooted in my soul, I grasp onto the last smidgen of *me* there is. I gyrate and spin with unsure steps. The jeers for me to strip echo through my armor, cracking through the wall. Filthy words are thrown at me like rocks. Breaking me. Piece by piece. When I open my eyes, I focus on blue eyes that pin me to the stage. The corner of his mouth lifts into a smirk, and a slight nod of his head gives me a small ounce of confidence I need to force myself to get through this.

I've done ballet all my life. I've danced before. Focusing on the thing I love, dancing, I do it. I make them whistle, I taunt them to beg for more and in that I find strength. I find my power and I'm reborn in that moment.

Two days ago, I danced for the first time. Samael comes to my room, he escorts me to 'work' then brings me back after my shift. He's good to me in an odd way. He never mentions Wolfe, even though I want to ask. I don't because I know the pain will only slice me wide open again.

I haven't been in the back rooms yet, but Sam has been training me every day. The harsher he is, the less my heart aches. The broken pieces of me fall away and all that's left is a shell.

Used, abandoned, and bruised.

Each day the pain becomes easier to handle. Pushing off my bed, I stand on shaky legs and make my way into the bathroom. In the dim light, I take in my appearance. The scars from the blade sit on my ribs and travel down to my hip, a reminder that I'm nothing in here. Just a pet.

"You look tired." A deep rumble comes from the doorway, and I startle, spinning to find Sam watching me. His gaze trained on my half-naked body. Blue pools pierce the scar on my side, as if he can will it away with just a look. But he can't. No one can.

"I am." My response is croaky at best, and I turn to regard myself again.

"There's something I need to talk to you about."

"What?" Turning to face him fully, I cross my arms in front of my chest and he smirks when his eyes fall to my breasts. "Don't be an asshole." I retort, knowing I shouldn't talk to him like that, but instead of darkness taking over his features, he offers me a smile.

"Come on, Firebird. Let's sit in the room. Put some goddamn

clothes on." Padding into my bedroom, I pull on a robe and settle on the bed, watching him intently.

"So?" I question slowly.

"Before he left, he asked me to look after you. I've tried my best. But now I need you to trust me. I'm about to do something I don't think anyone will see coming. Dax and I have come up with a way to get you out." He sounds so confident, but I don't let myself feel excitement. I can't get my hopes up when I don't know if this plan of theirs will work.

"How? I thought the only way to get out is if I'm dead." He nods in agreement, knowing that I'm right.

"I'll tell you soon, but I need to confess something else. Over the years, I always wanted him to get out of this place. But, with the family business in our blood, he was forced into this life. He is a good person, and it wasn't his choice to become a trainer. He wasn't supposed to get involved with you past the training either, but then you screwed that all up." He chuckles wryly. "My father threatened to kill you if he ever came back," he says matter-of-factly.

So many questions cross my mind. "My father knew, didn't he? It was his doing. The night in the study. Was it you? Did you drug me?" He stares at me for a while. Almost painfully. I can see the guilt in his gaze, but he schools his expression. He hides it so well. Sam doesn't need a mask because he's got the steel look down to a T.

"Our fathers came to an agreement. There was a contract long before you were born. I've seen it. Your father agreed to give Harlan his first-born daughter in exchange for the status of senator and to keep his real estate empire running smoothly. Do you know your father's been reelected every two years because of my father's influence? His first six year term my dad got him the seat. And each reelection was all Harlan Wolfe's doing. Madden Estates, your father's global conglomerate, is only successful because of Wolfe Enterprises. Did you know any of this?"

I shake my head as shock seeps through me, and I can't find the words to respond. I always suspected my father was involved in underhanded business dealings, but this is a new low. The man who raised me, who I trusted and loved, is as evil as the men who now hold me captive. "I spent my life being groomed to take over Madden Estates. Told I'd be next in line to run the company. And all this time, I was nothing to him." The words fall from my lips as the realization hits me full force, and I feel the tears burn my eyes.

Samael is quiet for a long moment. When he speaks again, his tone is hesitant. "You meant something to my brother. Everything perhaps. He loved you."

"I thought I was in love with him too, once. Have you ever been in love?" My gaze darts up, and I meet those cobalt eyes. He shakes his head and rises from the bed. In two long strides, he's at my dresser. When he presses the button for my little iPod docking station, the song "The After You" by Miakoda that streams through the speakers rips my heart from my chest.

"All I know about love is that it's a stupid emotion that only gets you hurt. Or killed. The life I live is a dark path. My brother saw it, my father knows it." His words drip with venom. Once again, his shield comes up closing himself off. Sam's confession is so fierce it slams into me painfully. "And now, my brother's fallen in love and he's gone."

"I'm sorry." The words fall from my mouth easily because I am. "You're right; it is my fau—"

"No, it wasn't." He turns to regard me then. "He's not made for this life. I am. Being the man who can withstand women's tears and still do the same thing to them day in and day out is not what my brother wants. He wants a life of solitude. A family."

Closing the distance between us, he sits beside me. The heat of his body, radiating tension, warms me. I shouldn't feel safe with a man like him, but I do. The man I love has a brother, a father, family. "Do you know where he is?" I ask, but he shakes his head.

"I'm going to get you out of here. I just need you to trust me." The look he pins me with then is stern, with a promise, a vow. Without a second thought, I nod.

"I do."

"Good girl." He stands and fastens the button of his suit jacket before making his way to the door. With a hand on the knob, he stops and drops his gaze to the floor. "Be ready in an hour. You've been requested for a party." And then he's gone.

My body is shaking with cold fear. Sam walked with me to the normal room five that I've become accustomed to, but once he left, another one of the men came to collect me and brought me to an area of the mansion I've never seen. It's almost an exact replica of the club, but on a smaller scale. A private wing, I'd guess.

"You'll fucking obey me, toy." The voice booms in the small room. I'd hoped I'd get a reprieve from him today, but sadly, I'm not that lucky. I drop to my knees on the black carpet and keep my eyes trained on the floor. The metal leash he always carries gets clipped to the collar around my neck. "Come." On all fours, I follow him, crawling like the pet I am. I thought it would be Harlan that requested me, but this is the stranger who raped me when I was bound in the dungeon. He and Harlan made me bleed that day.

As we weave our way through the mansion, I know where we're headed. The music from the party room echoes down the hallway, and as we near it, I can hear the men's voices over the deep thumping bass.

It's my first time doing this and I have a feeling tonight I'll be used until I pass out, maybe even after. Because that's what they did to me in the dungeon.

"Well, what do we have here?" A deep rumble cuts through

my thoughts and a hand, rough and calloused, reaches for my chin, tugging it up harshly. "She's a pretty one," he says to the man holding my leash, but stares at me.

"She's well trained," the old man says proudly, and I shiver. His voice is slurred, and I realize he's drunk already. "Come on, pet. Up on the table." He tugs the leash, pulling me toward the low mahogany table in the center of the room. I climb up with ease and sit back on my heels, waiting for my next command. The stranger who called me pretty crouches beside the table and meets my gaze. He's got kind blue eyes. I say kind, but what I really mean is that he's not scary. Not like the vile man who violated me.

"Do you like to play, little toy?" he asks, his tone laced with lust. I know their nicknames for the girls, *pet, toy*, Sam told me not to retort, just obey. So I do.

"Yes, Sir," I mumble. He reaches out and tugs at the clasp of my bra, unhooking it with one hand. The straps fall to my front, and when the material drops from my body, I hear the loud hiss from the others. I don't know how many there are, but I would guess six.

"So polite. Let's see how much that mouth can take." He rises, leaving me with a view of his shoes. They're shiny and black and remind me of the ones my father used to wear to work. The clink of a belt buckle alerts me that I'm about to be taken, and it won't be nice. "Eyes up." Lifting my gaze, I watch as he unzips his expensive slacks and drops them to his knees.

The thick ridge of his erection protrudes in my face, and I realize he wasn't wearing underwear. His big hand fists his shaft, taking the tip and running it over my lips. "Open your pretty, little mouth, kitten." I obey, like I was taught to do, and he slips the crown of his dick in my inviting mouth. "Fuck," he grunts in satisfaction. "Suck it like you do those lollipops you girls like so much." My cheeks cave in as I swallow him, sucking harder. His groan is evidence that I've been trained well.

He grips my head, fisting my long, red hair in thick fingers, and plunges himself deep down my throat. My gag reflex kicks in, and I choke on the tip as it hits me painfully. Spit drips from my chin and my eyes tear up. "Eyes up." Dragging my watery eyes up to him, I find a dark smirk on his lips.

As he continues fucking my face, I feel hands on me, ripping my panties from my frame and groping my flesh. The man before me grunts and his body locks before jets of release fill my mouth. When he finally pulls himself from my swollen lips, I'm dragged to the floor, directed to straddle a man with a mask on his face. I'm impaled on a thick cock and his hips rock up toward me as he fucks me bareback.

Just when I think I can't take anymore, another man nudges my tight, puckered entrance. Teasing it. I hear and feel the spit on my ass, and before the pain sears me, I retreat into my mind. The darkness I hold on to envelops me as I fight to keep myself sane.

As I try to grasp my soul and shield it from the filth and darkness, I pray for escape, beg for mercy, and plead for a reprieve.

"Just a toy, that's all you're good for. All you'll ever be."

"Tonight is the night." Samael barges into my room. The look on his face is fierce, and I realize what he means. I'm leaving tonight. "Get up. The bag I told you to pack, grab it and follow me." Without another word, he strides to the corner of the room and settles on the dresser as he always does.

Swiftly, I move to the closet and pull out the backpack I've had ready of some clothes I can wear while I figure out what's going to happen to me because there's one place I won't be returning to and that's my childhood home. "Where am I going?" I ask as we head down the hallway.

"You're going to leave with Dax and Theia. They'll be able to keep you safe. Axel is waiting at the club where he'll be able to take you to the apartment we have set up. You'll have a job and a place to stay. The rest is up to you."

"And..." I want to question him about his brother. If he knows where he is, but my words taper off.

"Listen to me, Firebird." Gripping my shoulders, he levels his gaze on mine. "I don't know where he is. We've not spoken in months. But I need you safe. If there's one thing I can do for my brother, it's to make sure the woman he loves has a life worth living, and even if he never knows what I've done, at least I know I've done one thing right and gotten you out. It's what he wanted. Be safe, Paige. I know you will. You're strong. Don't let assholes take advantage of you," he bites out. And just like that, he releases me and steps back. Those are the last words he says to me as we reach the door at the end of the long corridor.

It swings open and I'm met by Dax. My first impression from one glance is that this man is scary. If I walked into him on the street, I'd run the other way. He is easily taller than six feet with a full beard and tattoos covering his arms and neck reminding me of a dangerous biker or gang leader. But when he smiles, it's genuine. "Hello, little red. Let's get you outta here." He reaches for my bag, turns on his heel, and stalks to the waiting car.

With a last glance at Samael, I simply nod. "Thank you." One small smile is all he offers, and then he's gone. The car is waiting on the driveway, and when I slip into the backseat, there's a pixie of a girl sitting there. She regards me with affection, as if I'm her best friend and she's trying to soothe my ache. Perhaps she is, or she will.

"Hello, Red." Her sweet voice is like a salve to my agony, and I smile.

"Hi, I'm Paige." We shake hands when she tells me her name is Theia. Something about her is familiar, and when the light from outside slides across her face, I recognize it immediately.

She looks exactly like her brother. Samael. Which makes me wonder what their other brother looks like. He was different, dark brown eyes, tanned, whereas Theia is fair-skinned. My mind tries to create a mental picture of him, from what I have seen of his smile, but I can't and frustration has me sighing.

"You'll need a new name for your new life. Do you have one in mind?" She glances at me with curiosity. When Sam told me he'd be able to free me, that I had one chance to get out of hell, I sat back and reinvented myself. That night, I went through a list of names, and one that struck me as unique was Skyla. The meaning of it being scholar, or shield, and I knew right then, that's who I'd be. A scholar of life, learning to live in the real world, but a shield for all the pain and agony I've endured.

It's time to move on, and even if I must do it on my own, I'll find my strength. "Skyla," I murmur and glance at my new friend. Her sweet smile calms me. Her aura is like a healing mist, and I want to bask in it.

"I like it. Well, Skyla, welcome to your new life," she says happily as the car weaves its way to my new home. The destination unknown, but I know somewhere in the maelstrom I'll find my happiness.

And one day. Somehow. I'll find my Wolfe.

To Covet You

I bask in your light,
Your warmth is my life force,
My strength is your shield,
When our souls unite,
Our hearts meld as one

THIRTEEN

Kael

Six years later

It's been a year since the day that I confessed who I was to Paige.

I walked into Dax's club, Inferno, not realizing my whole life was about to change. Sitting in the front row and seeing my feisty Phoenix stepping onto the stage, I was completely and utterly floored. She'd matured in the most beautiful way.

When I left her in Caged, I knew she'd flourish and survive the nightmare. But when I saw her again after all those years, I knew I had to claim her.

There was no way I was going to let her go again.

I was a coward, it took me six months to confess who I was. I did it while I was deep inside her body. When she looked at me with anger, elation, love, frustration...every emotion tumbled around in those emerald orbs. And all I could do was wait for her to finally let out all of them and find the one that mattered most.

Forbidden Series Book Two   143

Love.

Her love for me.

She needed to know I wanted her. She needed to let me into her heart and mind. Not that I ever left, but with years of pent-up anger at me leaving, I was bound to have to fight my way into her life.

She never recognized me. I'd changed since I left Caged. My body was inked, my hair was long, and I grew a beard. My voice had changed after the months of torment my father put me through. I went back for her but she'd gone. He didn't appreciate his disowned son showing up.

He had me tortured for three months. Three men took turns beating me daily, I'd almost lost the will to live. My voice had cracked, changed, from the screaming I'd done. They'd cut my flesh for a confession on how I'd allowed her to escape. What got me through was the fact that I knew she was safe outside those walls.

When he released me again with a warning that if I ever came back he would kill me, I ran. It was only years later I found the strength to move back to New York. To find Axel and start a life close to my sister and Dax.

Axel inviting me to Inferno was a turning point. I'd found my long-lost Phoenix. Then I almost fucked it up again. The memory of that day still makes me shudder. If she had said no, I'm not sure what I would have done.

"It's your Wolfe, my sweet Phoenix," I murmur. Feeling her heart beating wildly in her chest, which thrums against mine. Recognition, shock, and anger swirl in her emerald eyes, piercing me with daggers. Straight to my heart. I did this. I hurt her again. She stares into my eyes, and she sees it. She sees me finally. She would never have recognized my voice after the torture my father put me through. It's huskier, deeper, I almost don't recognize it myself.

"It is you," she whispers in shock and awe. "How? Your voice, it's not the same. This doesn't make sense. Get the fuck off me!" she hisses angrily. "Now!" I obey, moving off her warm body, I watch her pace the room. When she stops and turns to me, she scowls. "Tell me the truth or get out!" She punches me in the chest. Her fire burning bright at my confession.

It's been five years since I last saw her. Since I left her in hell. Now I've finally found her and I'm not letting her go. My soul is in my hands. But my heart, it's in hers.

"Tell me, Kael!" Her voice echoes around us. Her body vibrates with controlled rage. I don't blame her. Those eyes I've missed looking into pierce me with a mixture of love, confusion, and anger.

I close the distance between us until I'm inches from her. "Listen to me, Phoenix," I murmur, hoping to calm her. "I need you to hear me out." I used to love when she begged me, now I'm the one pleading for her.

"Why the fuck should I listen to you? You lied!" I knew she'd be angry, so I wait. I don't move because she needs to hear me out. "Kael Wolfe?" I nod in response. "Jesus, I'm such an idiot. I should have figured it out." Her hand reaches for her panties, and I watch her tug them up her slender thighs.

"Paige, listen to me, I need you to just calm down." Lifting my hands in surrender, I try placating her, but she's having none of it. She shoots daggers at me with those beautiful eyes, and I don't blame her. For months I've been in here, making her feel, making her fall, and now that she has, I drop a bomb on her. It doesn't help that I'm still hard as fuck for her.

"Why the hell should I even give you the time of day?! Do you know what you did to me? Do you realize the pain you put me through for five long, agonizing years?" she retorts, spitting her words like venom. I deserve everything. Each word. The fury she pins me with slowly tightens my chest and breathing becomes difficult.

"I know—"

"No, you don't fucking know!" Her voice carries as she paces back and forth with her gaze flitting between me, the floor, and the window that overlooks the city. "You..." Her voice trails off, and she glances out the window. She's silent, and I think she's calmed, but when I take a step toward her, she spins on her heel. And that's when I see them. Tears. They stream silently down her cheeks, and they burn me like acid racing through my veins.

"Paige." My voice is a pained whisper, but her gaze doesn't meet mine.

"Fuck you, Kael Wolfe! You made me love you!"

I take another tentative step toward her, reaching for her hand, but she doesn't gift me hers. Instead, she rears her hand back and punches me in the chest, then the face. Her tiny fists fly left, right, left, and I let her. It will be the one time I ever allow a woman to hit me. Once the fight leaves her, she peeks at me.

"I hate you," she hisses, and I don't doubt she means every word.

"I love you." My confession has her laughing wryly.

"You don't love me. You didn't love me when you walked out and left me in that fucking hell."

"I loved you more then than I ever did. Paige, I never stopped loving you." This time, I reach for her and she allows me to hold her. To touch her. Pulling her into my arms, I inhale the scent of her, of us. It hangs heavy in the room. "These years without you have been the most difficult I've ever had to endure. Not having you close by, I felt as if I'd been crushed. My life stopped when I walked out, knowing I couldn't take you with me."

"You hurt me more than I ever could have imagined. I gave you everything, Kael. My heart, mind, my body... God, you were etched into my soul. Every breath I took was for you. Was because of you." Her words pierce me, slicing deep into my heart. Leaving me flayed at her mercy.

"Look at me, Phoenix." The words come out as an order, and as much as she should tell me to fuck off, she doesn't. Instead, she glances up, meeting my eyes with hers. "You're made for me. When I first saw you on stage here at Inferno, it felt as if I was alive again for the first time in years." Taking a deep breath, I search her gaze for hate, or anger, but I come up short. All I see is affection.

"Kael—"

"I walked in here asking for you every night knowing that if you knew it was me, you would hate me for what I put you through. But our time in that hell was real to me. When I felt your body mold around me, when I saw you come apart below me, when I watched you soar above me, those were the moments I've held on to all these years."

Her head drops into her hands, and she sighs. I want to go to her. To hold her. But I know I need to give her space. "The time with you was never a distraction. I gave you all of me because I loved you." Her words are sincere and I can take the distance no more. I stalk toward her, leaving no space between us. Nodding, I reach up, stroking my knuckles along her cheek, and she leans into my touch.

"Loved?" I question with my heart beating wildly in my chest.

"Yes, I loved you, but now..." Her words taper off, and emotion threatens to choke me. "This is more, Kael. This is so much more. I don't have words for it. I've always prayed you'd find me. I just..." She tugs free from my grasp and steps back. Her gaze never leaving mine.

"Paige, please, I need you. I can't live without you. Now that we've found each other, you can't tell me you don't want this? Us?" I implore her. I'm not averse to begging because I will if that's what it will take. There's nothing more I need in my life but her. Those eyes, her smile, those beautiful tits, and her incredible body. But most of all, I covet her heart. I always have. It was the one thing I was forbidden to want or take, but I did it anyway.

Now, as I stand here a free man, it's the only thing I'll accept.

She's silent for a long while, too long, in fact, before I close the distance between us. "Please, Paige," I ask again, my hands fisted at my sides, not wanting to force her hand, but needing to touch her. The ache is palpable.

I can see her mind racing with thoughts, her breathing is rapid, her chest rising and falling as everything crashes down around us and it feels like once again I'm burning in her blaze. She engulfs me in her heat, scorches me like a flame, consumes me like a wildfire.

And finally, when I'm seconds from losing the wavering grip I have *on my sanity completely, she throws me an olive branch. It isn't much, but to me, it's everything.*

The nightmares are our past, my dreams are our future, but right here with her stepping into my arms, this is my present. My gift from the only woman who's ever held my heart. And as she wraps her arms around me, tears falling from her eyes, I breathe for the first time in five years.

An ending.

A beginning.

She raises those emerald orbs in my direction, still red from tears. And she smiles.

Now that I have her, I'm never letting her go again. That same day, I went to Dax and told him I was taking my woman. He didn't have a choice because I didn't give him one. She was mine, and I wasn't leaving without her.

"Dax," I call the man who not only threw me out of my own home when my father disowned me, but who also helped my woman escape. He turns to me and piercing gray eyes meet mine.

"I never thought I'd see you in my club, Kael," he holds out a hand and I gladly shake it. If it weren't for him and my brother, I don't know where Paige would be.

"Neither did I. After everything that's happened, I didn't want to come in here. I didn't know what you did until she told me today." He nods. As much as anger kept me away from this place, it's love that brought me back.

"She's a special girl," he says with a smile.

"That she is. And that's why I'm taking her. She's no longer your employee. I won't have her in here dancing for men. I won't have her in those rooms doing something she escaped from." He glances at the girl I love as she makes her way over to us.

"I agree, Wolfe. I wouldn't want Theia up there either. I'm fine with her leaving, but the choice is ultimately hers." He's right. I know he is.

"Hey, are you two talking about me?" Paige sidles up to me, and I cocoon her with my body. She's still a waif, but she fits perfectly in the crook of my arm.

"We were. I was telling your ex-boss that we'll be leaving for Chicago soon." Her body stills, her gaze is trained on Dax, but he nods with a smile.

"Good luck to you both. Don't be strangers. You're welcome anytime." He leans in, pulling her into his arms, giving her a brotherly hug. "Look after this big asshole, would you?" He chuckles, slapping me on the back in a friendly gesture.

"Always," she whispers with a smile so bright, it's all I can see.

I helped her pack her bags and we moved to Chicago. I didn't give her a chance to say no. All she could do was relent. I know she misses the girls at Inferno. Over the almost five years she spent with Dax and Theia, she grew to love them, but I know there's one little lady she misses more than the others.

Dakota.

That was her only worry about leaving, their friendship.

Our lives in Chicago have given us a fresh start, and even

though I miss my best friend, I know Axel will be here soon with his girl. He's claimed the feisty little kitten, Dakota.

Life has taken on a routine, one I'm enjoying. I work on my painting contracts and she teaches dance classes at the local studio downtown, which she's been renting with an option to buy, while studying. Her focus has been on getting a Business Management degree, which I've paid for. Now that I'm in her life, she doesn't need to worry about a thing.

When I moved back to New York I got a surprising call from my sister. Apparently, a lawyer had contacted her with news for each of the Wolfe offspring. My mother had set up a fund for each of us, which they didn't find until much later.

We were meant to receive it when we turned eighteen, but something happened to the documentation, which I suspect had a lot to do with my father. My nest egg is big enough for us to live a comfortable life, and there's no concern about money. We can afford vacations, her schooling, and even the occasional five-star restaurant.

With my mind on dinner, I push open the door to the study. Before I step inside, I glance into the bright space and find her sprawled out on the sofa on her stomach, her legs bent at the knee. I get a small peek of red panties between smooth, creamy thighs.

She's deep in thought, reading an article on her new MacBook, and hasn't heard me enter. Her hair is pinned into a messy bun, strands of long red waves tumbling from the clip, teasing her neck and back.

The air in the room slowly heats as I lean against the doorjamb, arms crossed with my eyes fixated on her.

"Are you going to stand there all day?" she quips playfully, rolling over to regard me. The short white T-shirt she's wearing rides up, and I'm greeted with not only her intense emerald eyes, but also the bright red lace panties that cup her sweet, little pussy.

"You going to taunt me with those all day?" I lift my chin, gesturing at her sheer panties. Her green gaze darts down and she giggles.

"I figured you'd come home after a long day and need a distraction?" She shrugs innocently, but I know there's nothing innocent about her. As much as I'd love to take her, I decided today we need to have a long talk before anything else.

I want her to tell me about the events that took place after I left. We've not had the talk about what she went through. When I did bring it up a month ago, she froze and told me she wasn't ready to delve into those memories. So far, I've decided to give her time. We're still learning to be with each other outside of the hell we met in.

"I do need a distraction, Phoenix, but not in the way you think." Her face falls and I see the worry etch itself all over it. "I think you know what we need to do." My no-nonsense tone is enough to have her biting down on that plump lower lip.

"I know," she sighs. Scooting over, she watches me under dark lashes. As soon as I'm settled on the sofa beside her, she crawls into my lap. Her body molds to mine, fitting like we're two intricately designed pieces of one mosaic. All our colorful and broken fragments come together, making one beautiful glass canvas, completely transparent, and yet so fragile.

"Tell me, baby. I've got you. I'm never letting you go again, but you need to tell me what happened. Or I'm going to find my brother and kill him." Since I walked out on him, I hadn't looked back once. But when he called asking for help with his girl, I knew I had to put everything behind me and go to him and that was the last time we spoke. It was over a year ago and now Freya and Sam are together, happily living their life.

"No, Sam saved me, Kael." Her words ring true to what Dax told me. "He... I guess for you to understand, you'll need to hear it all." She sighs, and I tug her closer. My thumb circles the smooth skin over her shoulder as she starts her story. She begins to re-live her horrific past at the hands of my father and the "clients." How she would shut herself off just to survive. Just to deal with the pain of having lost me. At one point, she shudders in my arms, and I feel my self-control slip.

The need to hurt someone, to kill someone runs rife through my blood like poison.

"Baby—" I murmur, but she cuts me off and continues.

She turns her head to regard me, planting a soft kiss on my

cheek. She reaches up to stroke my beard. Her normally emerald eyes are dark, reminding me of the color of leaves from an oak tree.

With a deep breath, she starts again. "One night, Sam stumbled into my room. I thought he was drunk. He climbed into my bed and I waited on the pain, but none came. I waited for him to touch me, or fuck me, or something, but he didn't. He just lay there for what felt like hours in the dark, in silence. When I finally rolled over to regard him, his blue eyes met mine, and we spoke. He told me about growing up with you, about how he begged Harlan not to let you get into that life, but it was in your destiny or whatever. He told me the truth about how he wanted me that night, but he knew I was yours. He wasn't a monster, he was hurting. When you left, he changed. Something inside him snapped, the next day he came into my room and told me he was going to get me out."

Jolting upright, I grip Paige to me, lifting her and placing her on my lap so she's straddling me. "Dax told me most of that, but I needed to hear it from you."

She nods. "Samael and Dax helped me escape. I worked at Inferno until you walked in and found me. I know you've not spoken to him since you helped him with Freya, but I think it's time we went there, or just called them." Her gaze drops and I know she's hiding something. "I don't know, Kael, I feel as if I owe him my life. He..."

Her words taper off and she fidgets with the hem of her T-shirt. I realize she's still not telling me everything. "Baby, look at me." It's a command and she complies. "Good girl. Tell me what you're hiding."

Emotions blaze like wildfire in those teary pools. "I don't think—"

"No, you shouldn't. I'd like you to tell me."

"Before Sam could get me out, I... I had a client. Although, he wasn't a client..." She falls silent. The tension radiating from her body has me vibrating with rage, and I don't even know why yet. "He came into the room one day, Sam, and he told me to get ready. He didn't look happy and fear crept in. When I asked him why, he only uttered, *'I wish I could have saved you from this, Firebird,'* and then he left. An hour later, I was dressed and had just finished my hair when he entered my room. As we walked down the hallway, I knew. Something deep in my gut slowly chewed at me. Sam looked at me before he opened the door to a room I'd never been in and whispered in my ear to *'remember where your heart lies'* before he ushered me into the wolves' den."

Those final words send me reeling. My body stills, tenses to the point of pain, and my heart thuds. It fucking fights its way out of my chest, and I tighten my hold on her so much that I hear her gasping for air. Agony slices through me, my blood boils, and torment rattles my bones when I realize what she's telling me.

"Paige, tell me what happened. Now." Each word is

annunciated like a threat. A vow. I would kill him if my brother hadn't already taken the initiative. I wouldn't need weapons because I'd rip him apart. Easily, I'd tear off his skin with the whips he used on us as children, and on the women he abused. I wish I could see him bleed out before me. "Tell me, Paige."

I shouldn't ask.

She shouldn't tell me.

But she will. She must.

I must know.

"He... Your father was there. But there's something else that not even Sam knows." She blinks, and I feel like I've been punched in the gut. Tears stream down her flushed cheeks. "Harlan took me that night. There was a video recording of it. He told me he'd break me for loving you, for making you act out and for making you covet a whore. But there was another man with a mask. They both..."

"Jesus, baby. Look at me please." She does, gifting me with those big green eyes. Those precious gems that sparkle with emotion. As much as I want her to hate me, hate my family, I don't see that emotion anywhere on her face. All I see is love. For me.

"They broke me. For twenty-four hours, both fucked me violently. I was choked and whipped." Her words are strangled as she gasps for breath, recalling what those sick, vile monsters did to her. "They forced themselves inside me before I was ready.

I bled so much, I thought I'd die. Since you were gone, I wished for death."

Those words gut me, they fucking slice through me like a blade opening me to her.

"Every day. I just didn't feel like I could live and in that moment, I prayed for it. My fight was washed away by the tears they ripped from me. My body became nothing. My heart, as much as it longed for you, it shattered. And my soul, it filled with darkness. This here..." She lifts the hem of her top and stands until I finally see the marks hidden by the ink. I wondered why she was always so quick to hide her tattoo from me, but I never examined her properly. I didn't see the scars below the Phoenix tattooed on her hip. The *W*, which my father must have carved into her skin.

"Jesus, Paige," I bite out the rage fueled words. "I came back for you too late. I was too fucking late." My heart constricts at the memory of entering the property and finding four guards waiting for me. Of my father laughing, telling me she's gone.

Her gaze snaps to mine and she gasps. "You came back for me?" Meeting her gaze, I nod. "And I had already left. They'd gotten me out."

"Yes, you had been gone for about a month already. I didn't realize it because as soon as I got onto the property, I was captured. I'm lucky to be alive. I didn't even get to talk to Sam or Dax so I didn't know where you were." I realize that all these years I was angry at my brother, but all he did was save my girl.

"He told me he didn't know where you were. But he said if you knew about his plan, it wouldn't work. He planned my escape with Dax, who in turn, gave me a job when I got out. I did all those things at Inferno because I was angry at you. I didn't know you came back, I thought you didn't care."

"I'm so sorry I didn't come back sooner. I was a mess." My frustration that I wasn't there to save her from the torture I know she endured rings clear in my words.

"For too long my life wasn't my own and when I lost you..."

"Kael," she breathes my name, leaning in until her lips are an inch from mine. "I was a young girl who didn't know much about love. But when I let you in, it wasn't only into my body. You claimed every part of me. When you walked out of that house, you had my heart. You've always had it." Her confession stills me before I close the remaining inch between us and I claim her mouth. Out tongues duel, they dance with more than just a kiss. I consume her breaths as she steals mine.

FOURTEEN

Kael

When he breaks the kiss I'm dizzy, it feels as if I'm drunk. Everything he's ever done to me has left me with lasting memories. Yes, we've been through some dark times. Our path was never easy, but we made it through.

I've been hesitant about trying more intense play since we found each other again. After being in that house, using my body to forget the pain, I don't know how I'll handle being bound, blindfolded and dominated.

When I was at Inferno, I played the part, but this feels different. With Kael I have all those memories racing back, but I think it's time to test the waters. To see if I can handle more.

"I wish we had a better start," he says, and sadness flickers in his eyes.

"I do too, but we are stronger for it. I know I am. Yes, there are times it still haunts me. That house, those men, the pain... Perhaps I'll never get over it completely, but I want to try." The words come easily when I lose myself in his deep brown eyes.

"What do you mean?"

"There's something we do need to talk about." He stares at me causally, as butterflies awaken in my belly. I don't know why I'm nervous. I should just be honest and tell him I'm ready to play again. For him to dominate me. "So, uhm..." I mumble while stroking his chest absentmindedly. The silence is deafening and I'm sure he can hear my heart beating wildly at the thought of what I'm about to ask. *Thud. Thud. Thud.*

He pins his chocolate gaze on me in curiosity. "What's wrong, Paige?" His question is wary at best and he should be because this isn't going to be easy.

"Well, I was just thinking it's been a long time that we've had time to experiment, or had time to be...I mean I haven't really been with anyone I cared for. The past year since you found me has given me more confidence. Being submissive to someone was, and still is, difficult for me."

"Paige, you know as much as I'd like to take you and play out a scene, I don't want you to do it because of me. I need you to be comfortable. You've been through too much for us to even consider—"

"That's... I mean..." Sighing, I push off his lap. He watches me closely as I pad over to the small cabinet, where I know he's hidden the pretty item that he's probably dying to see on my neck. I thought my fear would have it lost forever, but when I found it, I knew I needed to be strong enough to wear it.

"What are you doing?"

I don't respond, instead, I open the safe and pull out the sleek silver box. "Were you ever going to give this to me?" When his dark gaze falls on the box, a small smirk lifts the corner of his mouth.

"Were you snooping?" he growls, pushing off the sofa and sauntering over to me with his confident stride. Once we're close, he takes the box and snaps it open. "Do you want this?" He sounds unsure. I was scared last week. Fuck I was afraid this morning, but after telling him everything, I can't deny how much I want and need him.

"I want you, Kael."

"You know what this means, Phoenix?" he murmurs the nickname he gave me when he found me at Inferno. I nod. He only calls me that pet name when we're about to play and I'm tingling with anticipation already.

As much as I'm wary and afraid. I need to try. He needs this and so do I. It's part of who I am. Who he is. "Yes," I affirm with confidence that I don't fully feel. I shouldn't enjoy this lifestyle. I shouldn't get wet and needy when he spanks me or binds me to the bed.

Guilt sits heavily in my chest. Confusion seeps into my veins and disgust at what I endured still lingers. I want Kael to take it away. I want him to teach me to love who I am, what I am. His submissive.

Meeting his gaze again, I wait. He's weighing what to do next, I recognize the flicker in his eyes as they flit between me and the silver choker with a small pendant hanging from it. The collar he bought when we first moved to Chicago. I only know this because I found it then, but I was too scared to ever think of being owned again.

"If this is what you want, if you're sure, then I'll collar you, Phoenix. I want you. I want to own you. Mind, body, and soul. But more than that, I want your heart. All of it."

"And I want you," I murmur, dropping to my knees and offering him my presentation pose. Even though I'm not naked, the action allows me to bare my soul to him. A hiss of approval falls from his mouth.

He's tentative, I can tell by his posture and the way he regards me. But when I glance up, it's all there. Everything he's hidden since we found each other again. And I want it. I want the monster he hides. "Fuck you're so beautiful submitting for me."

"I'm yours," I whisper.

"I want you in the bedroom, naked, kneeling, present yourself to me. We'll play a scene. Once you're coming on my mouth, fingers, and cock, I'll know you're ready. Then and only then will I collar you." With that, he turns and leaves me on the floor. I know what he's doing. He's not taking control just yet. He's allowing me a choice. Something I never had when we were together in Caged.

Rising, I pad to our bedroom knowing exactly what I want. It's in my heart. I'm always going to be his. And it's time to give him my all.

FIFTEEN

Kael

OPENING THE FRIDGE, I PULL OUT THE ICE TRAY. I'M intrigued by my little firebird.

She's given me trust—she's given me *everything*—but her nervousness about giving this lifestyle another try when she's been through so much already has only cemented the fact that I want her collared. Owned by me and only me. And I can't wait to see how beautiful her slender neck looks with that collar.

Stalking into our bedroom, I find my little Phoenix kneeling as I've requested. "Have you thought about what you asked for?" I ask and I watch her nod silently. "Answer me, I need words, Phoenix."

"Yes, Sir."

"And what's your conclusion?" I question, setting the ice tray on the cabinet which holds our toys.

She snaps her gaze to me and furrows her pretty brows. "What do you mean?"

Her confusion is adorable. "When you asked to be collared, you realize it means you relinquish all control in the bedroom.

That means I will be your Master, your Dominant." I love teaching her. I know she's not new to this life, but I want our future to be different than our history. This won't be easy for her, but with her trust in me, I'll make sure her mind and body are only focused on the here and now. I want to not only feel the pleasure, but to be consumed by it. By me.

"Yes, Sir. Like I said, I'm yours. Yes, I'm nervous. I'm scared beyond all reasoning, but this is who I am and if I don't take a step forward, I'll always be stuck in the past," she murmurs. Her fingers fidget with the thin band of the ring I bought her. It's not the one I wanted, but that one will come soon enough.

"Yes, you're mine. And you will be scared, but remember, I'm not them. Your pleasure is my only concern with this scene. Now tell me, what are your thoughts on the scene? Do you want a safe word?" Her gaze darts up to me, I want to punish her for it, but I restrain myself. I need to take it slow.

"I trust you. I don't need a safe word." Sometimes her strength astounds me.

"Are you sure, Phoenix?"

"Yes, Sir." She smiles up at me, her emerald eyes sparkling like gems.

Nodding, I saunter over to her and hold out my hand. "Good girl." My murmur sends a small shiver over her as she slips her hand in mine. I tug her to stand and reach up to cup her face in my hands. "Now, I want you bent over the table. Let me spank that pretty, creamy ass."

She opens her mouth to say something, but I pin her with a stern look, watching her shrink into the submissive I love. She heads over to the varnished oak table in the corner of the room. She bends over it, her beautiful breasts flat against the top, her ass taunting me from her stance.

Pressing the button on our stereo, the iPod lights up and I know the song I'm going to use. "The Phoenix" by Fall Out Boy.

"Open those pretty legs," I command, my dominant voice coming across, booming around us. She obeys without a sound, and I head over to grab the spreader bar. My cock throbs against my zipper just waiting to be let loose and drive into her.

When I head back to her, I take in the beautiful woman before me, open and waiting for me. With two clicks, I fasten the locks on each ankle, immobilizing her. Then, as I proceed to cuff her to the silver rings on the opposite end of the table, she murmurs softly, "I'm sorry it took so long for us to get back here."

"What? Phoenix, you have nothing to be sorry about."

She nods in understanding. Grabbing my smooth, red leather flogger, I tease it over her skin. Her body is a temple—one I'll worship forever. I will marry her very soon. I want to watch her supple body change as she bears my children. To see her pregnant would be a dream come true.

Lifting my hand with the flogger, I rain down swat after swat on her ass. The thin tendrils lick at her pussy and her skin tinges with a light dusting of pink. Her legs tremble, but I don't stop until I reach twenty.

"You're beautiful wearing my mark," I whisper. Reaching for her, I lightly stroke her spine from her neck, down to her incredible ass. She wiggles playfully, and I lower my hand, dipping into her core. Drenched. She's slick with desire, ready for me to plunge into her. "Is this what you wanted, little bird? Do you like me owning you? Marking you as mine?" I murmur while I tease her sweet little cunt.

"Yes, Kael, please fuck me. Please."

"Oh, I will, Phoenix. But our scene isn't over yet." I stroll over to the ice tray and grab two blocks. Once I'm behind her, I drop to my knees. Her scent is intoxicating. My mouth waters to taste her. "Yell stop if you feel like you need to," I growl, but she doesn't say anything. A mere whimper and her legs tremble. Using both blocks, I trail them over her heated pink ass.

"Oh God!" Her cries echo loudly through our bedroom, but I ignore her, continuing my trail down to her glistening little cunt. Teasing it with the ice, her body quivers, and she tugs on her restraints. "Fuck, Kael. Sir, please, anything. Please. Oh god." The whimpers only spur me on to continue, and as the ice melts, I lean in and lick her from her hardened little clit to that beautiful puckered hole I'm going to fuck.

My ministrations on her body only have her mewling louder. "Are you thinking about my collar around your pretty neck,

Phoenix?" I bite out, then continue lapping at her pussy. When she doesn't answer, I reach up and circle her clit, tugging on it. "I asked you a question. Are you going to allow me to collar you?"

"Yes, yes, please. Let me come please," she begs. I love hearing her beg.

"Do you think you've earned the right to come, Phoenix?" This time, I drive two fingers into her and I know she's close because her body pulses around me. With my other hand, I swat her ass, leaving my bright pink handprint on it.

"Please, Sir. Let me come. I want your collar. Own me. Anything please, just let me come." Another swat as I drive my fingers into her. Inserting a third finger, she cries out so loud, I'm sure our neighbors can hear her.

"I think you've possibly earned one orgasm, little bird. You're my pet. Mine."

"Yes, yes, yes. I am, I am." Crooking my fingers, I rub her sweet spot. "Fuck please, Kael, let me come, please."

Pulling my digits from her, I rise to my feet. "You'll only come when my dick is inside you. Because I have to remind you that your body is mine." Shoving my jeans down, I fist my dick and ram inside her so hard, she screams my name louder than anything I've ever heard. The sound is wretched from her gut, from her very core, and I smirk.

My body slams against her bound figure harder and harder, pressing her into the oak table. My release locks my body and I bite out. "Come with me, pet. My Firebird. My fucking Phoenix."

And she does. Her release splinters her into a thousand tiny pieces and I put her back together. Not perfect, not flawless, but mine. And together, we find bliss.

Two days have passed since I collared her and Paige has been happy, content. Our session was one of the most powerful sessions we've had, but we're stronger for it. The woman is utter perfection. "They're almost here. I've missed her so much," she states enthusiastically, as she flops onto the sofa. Her excitement at seeing her best friend is adorable.

Even at twenty-six, as responsible and intelligent as she is she still has that childlike excitement for life and everything in it. After all the horrors she faced, she's indeed risen from the ashes, and that makes me love her even more. With her passion for her business, teaching children ballet and dance, as well as older women pole dancing as a form of fitness she's managed to face the future with positivity.

The doorbell dings alerting us to our visitors, and I push off the sofa, but Paige is bolting to the door before I've even taken a step. Two loud voices echo through our living room as the girls come face to face for the first time in months.

Once I reach the entrance, I find them embracing and

blubbering. Dragging my gaze away from them and over to my best friend, I offer a hand, pulling him into a brotherly hug. "Axe. It's been too long."

"Man, it's good to see you again." He grins, and I can see the happiness in his eyes. He's found love with Dakota and I'm glad he's got a good woman. We both drop our hands, and Dakota circles her arms around my waist.

"I'm so happy to be here. New York isn't the same without you guys," she says into my shirt, and I can't help but return her embrace. Paige wraps her arms around Axel. I know he was there for here when I wasn't. The friendship between them is clear.

"It's good to have you here, Kota. Come on, let's get some drinks," I offer, and we head into the kitchen. I grab the Macallan, and pour double shots in two tumblers. Once our drinks are ready, I grab a bottle of wine for the girls and fill two wine goblets.

We fall into an easy rhythm, chatting. I'm relaxed after a couple of whiskies. Axel and I are sitting comfortably in the living room when he turns to me, his expression serious.

"Sam said he's made sure there are no links to Paige and your father or Caged. Dax is helping him, but there's something else," he says, dropping his voice to a whisper.

"I didn't realize you were working for my brother. What's he found out?"

He glances toward the kitchen where the girls have disappeared to make sure it's safe, then back at me. "He thinks

Harkin is alive."

"That doesn't make sense, my uncle died when we were in college." This is news to me. I haven't spoken to Sam in a while, and he's not contacted me about it.

"There's documents confirming his body was never found. And..." his voice tapers off which intrigues me further.

"What is it, Axe?"

"We think Harkin had a kid," he confesses.

"A kid? With who? I don't remember any cousins around the mansion." He shifts his attention from the glass to me with a serious expression.

"As soon as we get back I'm meeting with Dax to figure shit out. Sam did say he would call you," he responds.

Nodding, I gulp the whiskey, pondering on what he's just told me. Before I can say any more, two lithe bodies join us, and when we turn to regard them, the sight nearly knocks me off my damn feet.

Axel and I sit back, drinks in hand, watching the scene play out. Both girls, dressed in black lingerie that's hugging their exquisite curves, caress and taunt each other. A Kitten and a Phoenix, playing together like two naughty schoolgirls.

Alone, they're perfection. Together they're every man's wet dream.

Their giggles echo sweetly through the room. Paige's hand snakes between Dakota's thighs and a whimper dripping with desire falls from the brunette's lips. "Girls," Axel rumbles beside me, and they both stop, dragging their gazes over to us. "Let's see how much you missed each other. Sixty-nine for us. Get each other nice and wet."

Svelte bodies move on the plush carpet, and I watch in awe as Dakota tugs my firebird's panties down her long legs. Paige in turn does the same and now they're both bare below. "How about you both get those pretty breasts out too," I suggest and they giggle in response. Once they're both naked the show starts as they get comfortable on the floor in the sixty-nine position. It didn't matter what position we had our girls in, they would always belong to us.

Fucking exquisite.

Their mouths go to work, and the soft moaning sounds have me solid behind the zipper of my jeans. After the loss she suffered in her life—first her family and then me—she closed off from everyone. But I can only thank my lucky stars that she found a friendship as strong as the one she has with Kota.

A connection like that comes once in a lifetime, and I can't help but smile when I see them not only chatter like teenagers, but also play like this. The sex between the girls is beautiful, a real connection. It's not just fucking for the sake of it.

"Paige is quite a stunner. Dakota loves her very much," Axel says from beside me.

"As does Phoenix. She's always talking about Kota. I wouldn't have pegged her as bi when I trained her." His blue gaze settles on me in understanding, and I sip my whiskey before responding. "I was Paige's first and only, until I left that place, as you now know." I glance at him and he nods. He glances back at the girls who are feasting on each other like they're candy. "Fuck, I think we need to get in there. They're having way too much fun," I bite out. He chuckles and pushes off the sofa as we make our way to our two beauties.

"Stop." His authoritative tone rumbles in the air, and they both startle and stare at us.

"But, Axe—" Dakota whines, which earns her a glare. She quickly moves off my Phoenix and they both kneel before us on the carpet with mouths glistening. I lean in and trace my girl's lips with my tongue, tasting the sweetness of the brunette.

"She's delectable." I reach for the leash hanging between Paige's breasts and tug her forward. "You want to play, Firebird?" She nods, peering up at me through thick lashes that are dark with mascara. "Good girl."

I pull my T-shirt up and over my head. Axel follows suit, tugging his Guns 'n Roses tee off and tossing it to the floor. "I'm sure you're both fully versed in what you need to do now," he quips. Their slender fingers dart up and rid us of our jeans and boxer briefs. In tandem, their pretty mouths go to work, and I can't help groaning at how well Paige swallows my cock down her throat. She's like a hungry tigress as her lips wrap around the base. Her green, glistening eyes peek up at me, and the sight has me groaning. I'm so close. She knows exactly what to do and when to do it. My body is tense as I try to hold on to the release that's already teasing me.

Another two slurps and I'm pulling her to her feet. "Enough. Time for you ladies to get fucked." Those emerald pools shimmer in the dim light, and she smirks, knowing full well she's going to get a treat.

Axel proceeds to sit back on the plush sofa and gets his kitten to straddle him while facing us. My girl kneels between Axel's thighs, and I position myself behind her.

The sight of Dakota's tight little ass being filled is enough to set me off. I guide my cock into Paige's drenched pussy. "Eat her cunt, Phoenix," I order, and my girl obeys beautifully, lapping at the smooth, bare slit of her best friend. We start moving in sync, and I watch as Axel taunts his girl's nipples and clamps them with the silver chains the girls brought in before their little show, causing her to cry out loud.

The wet sounds of Paige eating the little brunette are the sexiest thing I've ever fucking heard. My hips ram into my woman, who in turn devours Dakota's pussy, causing her to cry out again and again. The deep, feral growls of Axel as he slams into his girl's ass echo around us like a symphony of lust, desire, and sex. We've played before, but this is so much more. Emotion hangs in the air, and I know we'll always be this way. The four of us are friends. We're family. We're soul mates. My hips roll, bucking into the tight heat of my girl, and I can't hold on much longer.

I reach for the chains hanging from Dakota and tug on her nipple clamps as a shudder wracks her body. "So beautiful. Isn't she baby?" I question, spanking my firebird's ass hard as she yelps into her friend's little cunt. I reach for my girl's nipples, tugging them roughly, pulling them enough to send pain and pleasure coursing through her as her orgasm nears.

"Fuck, I'm going to come," Axel growls.

"Yes, please, Sir!" Dakota cries as he pulls on the clamps. My hand snakes between Phoenix's thighs, tweaking her clit until she's exploding on my cock and my body locks behind her.

The melody of our fucking detonates us all as we find exquisite release with each other, our bodies molding together in a beautiful piece of art. Skin slick with sweat, moans and whimpers slowly die as we all hold on to the euphoria for a little while longer.

It's one of the most intense orgasms I've ever experienced with others around, and with my body being connected to Paige's, it's everything.

SIXTEEN

Paige

"HEY MY BABE." DAKOTA SIDLES UP TO ME IN THE KITCHEN wearing a tiny black robe. "Your man is lovely," she whispers in my ear, even though the guys are in the living room and have the television on so loud, it's like I'm at the concert they currently have playing.

"I know. It took us a while to get back to a normal relationship, if you can call it that. I told him I wanted more, and he gave me this," I say, pointing to the thin silver choker around my neck.

Her giggle is enough to have me laughing too. "Are you sure you're ready to submit?" she asks and I nod with confidence. "I'm pleased. You needed stability and he's your rock." Being open about our lifestyle isn't easy, but with her, I know she gets it. It's like having a sister to confide in. Even though we're the same age, I feel protective of her.

"You two misbehaving again?" Axel's deep voice startles us both from the entrance of the kitchen. The dark blue of his T-shirt deepens the blue of his piercing eyes. Lifting one brow, his gaze flits between us in question, and I can't stifle my laugh.

"Come on, Axe. We're just having some girl time," Dakota whines beside me, and we notice another formidable figure joining Axel in the doorway.

Two men, complete opposites, but so alike.

"Yeah, come on, Axel..." I drag his name out slowly, and the blue in his eyes darkens considerably.

"Do you two need a spanking already?" Kael saunters into the kitchen, perching himself on the stool near the fridge. "I think they need a little girly time. I'd say we should take this to the hot tub with some champagne. Don't you think, Phoenix?"

Dakota snaps her gaze to mine, and it's as if our minds are one because the expression on her face tells me we just had the same idea. "I think my Kota would like to join me in the water." I lean in and whisper in her ear, "How about we have a few drinks and then taunt them a little?"

We stare at them for a moment then stroll past two pairs of hungry eyes with a bottle of bubbly and our flutes. The hot tub is out on the second-floor deck, which has an incredible view of the city.

Only a minute passes before the guys join us, both dressed only in their briefs, and from what I can tell, they're both very happy we're here.

"You two look delicious all wet," Axel quips with that side smirk that deepens the dimple in his cheek. Both men join us and seat themselves in the bubbly water. The spray jets out at random sections, which massage or tickle, depending on the pressure.

"Time to toast." Kael pops the cork and fills the flutes, while Axel hands us ours. "To new and old friends, and to forever." We clink glasses. Taking a sip of the cold alcohol, I sit back, and we settle into easy conversation.

"Action time," Kota whispers, and I nod. Both men are deep in conversation about business deals or something, but as soon as we turn and lean in, our lips touching, all chatter ceases. I feel two pairs of eyes, burning into my side, as Dakota's tongue and mine swirl alongside each other.

Our moans and whimpers are the only sounds surrounding us. I reach for her breasts, teasing the hardened buds between my thumb and forefinger. Her hands trail down my hips, tugging me against her. We're slippery, and based on a quick glance at the two men, I'd say our plan is working perfectly.

They're both entranced. I pull her up along with me, and when we stand, the water cascades down our legs. "Sit, Kota. You're first." I wink and she settles on the edge, gripping the wood to keep herself steady. I spread her slender legs and lean in, teasing her with feather light kisses on her inner thighs. "My perfect little, K," I moan, glancing up to find her eyes hooded.

"Please, Phoenix," she whimpers, and I can't deny her. My mouth latches on to her bare slit, and I lick and taste the sweetness of her. She leans back, her legs splayed almost lewdly, as I suck on her clit, teasing my fingers into her. "Oh, oh, shit." Her body pulses around my fingers and I know she's close. I know what she needs, so I bite down on her little nub and crook my fingers to stroke her sweet spot and she flies apart under my touch. "Shit, shit, oh, shit!" Her cries echo around us, but we're both lost in our pleasure.

In our own bubble.

I continue licking her until she slowly descends from her high. "You'll kill me, Little Red." She giggles down at me. Without casting a glance at the boys, we swap places, and she settles between my thighs. Her tongue works magic on me, and I'm gripping the edge of the Jacuzzi like a fucking lifeline.

Her mouth taunts and teases as she suckles my throbbing clit. Her fingers slide into me, pumping in and out, slow and meticulous. My release is so close I can taste it, when she suddenly curls her two fingers inside me, pressing down on my G-spot, which sends me spiraling into oblivion. "Fuck, God, Dakota!" I cry out as my body locks and she continues plunging her digits into me.

My body trembles and when I open my eyes, Dakota's pretty caramel ones are glistening along with her lips. "I love you, Phoenix."

"I love you too, Kitten."

"You two are fucking beautiful." My man's deep voice is akin to a growl. We both turn to find Kael and Axel staring at us with their fists around thick, angry erections. It's the hottest thing I've ever seen. "How about you both come and show us a little attention too."

"I think the little Kitten and Phoenix need to show us some love before they get those sexy asses spanked till they're bright red," Axel grunts in a rough tone. When these two hot men are sitting naked with their dicks in hand, we're not going to deny them.

Having Dakota here has allowed me to vent, rant, and spill secrets. Over the years we'd spent at Inferno together, I'd become accustomed to her being around, so when I left, it took some time getting used to not seeing her every day. There's always been this innate need in me to care for others, and when I first laid eyes on the little Kitten, I knew we'd be best friends. That we'd be *soul sisters*. It might sound cliché, or even hipster, but it's true. We know each other. We finish each other's sentences, almost like twins.

Conversation flows between the four of us. It's been an hour since we got into the hot tub, and our champagne is long since finished. Dakota and Kael are deep in conversation, so I silently slip out of the water and pad into the kitchen. Opening the wine cooler, I grab the chilled bottle of sauvignon and proceed to uncork it when I hear soft footfalls. "Did you follow me for a quickie?" I question, giggling. "You shouldn't leave our guests alone out there, baby..."

My voice drops when I lift my gaze and am met with the eyes of one of my closest friends. I'm still thankful to him for all he did for me after I left Caged. His deep blue eyes pierce me. A small smile lifts the corner of his mouth as he holds me hostage with an intense stare. "I suppose you were expecting someone else?" he quips with a gesture toward the door, and I nod.

"I was. I'm sorry. I thought he followed me." Dropping my gaze, I focus on the bottle in my hands as I pick at the label. Axel nears me and places his index finger under my chin, making me meet his searing gaze. There isn't any lust or desire in his eyes, instead they're filled with concern, though I'm not sure why.

"I'd like you to look at me," he requests kindly with another smile. "You're an incredible woman, Paige. My girl loves you, and in turn that means I love you too. You've given Dakota more than I can ever thank you for."

"You better treat her right, Mr. Knight," I warn. "Because I will kill you if you hurt her." My warning has him chuckling and he pulls me in for a hug.

"I'll never hurt her. And you, my sweet Firebird, you have my protection if you ever need it." He steps back, offering me a warm smile. "Now let's get back to those two."

Since my best friend left yesterday, I've been focused on my classes. I miss her when she's in New York, but I know she and Axel need time together. When he told me how he feels about her, my heart filled with happiness. She needs a strong man to care for her. Her past is much like mine, filled with heartache.

Our stories have an intermingling storyline in the sense that we've both faced atrocities. And even through everything life has thrown at us, we've managed to pull each other out of darkness before. The support of our friendship has given us strength. I will always make sure she doesn't spiral into that abyss again.

Stepping into the studio, I take in the small class waiting for me. "Hi girls, you ready to dance?" I drop my purse on the floor near the mirror and the five girls nod in unison.

"Yes, Miss Paige!" they all shout out excitedly. They're here for hip-hop classes and are always overly enthusiastic about class.

"Good. Who's been practicing?" They all raise their hands, and I smile, pushing the Play button on the stereo. The song comes through the speakers, and squealing erupts over the sound of the song choice. Thirteen-year-old girls all squeal when it comes to the Biebs. "Okay, I want to see your forms. Let's get those counts right. Remember, it's an eight count." They nod and as the song starts, they get into routine and I watch with pride as they fall into step beside each other.

It's been a long while since I felt such pride. Yes, teaching wasn't what I thought I'd end up doing, but seeing them so excited to learn how to dance makes me smile. I sit back and wonder if I'll ever have children one day. It's something Kael and I haven't really spoken about, but I know I'd love to have little Wolfe's running around. And that brings my thoughts to marriage.

To be Mrs. Wolfe one day is something I want. I know Sam and Freya are married now, which makes me wonder why Kael hasn't asked me yet. I don't want to rush into it, but I know in my heart I'm ready. If he asked me today, I'd say yes. There's no doubt in my mind that he's my forever. He's always been the man embedded in my heart, and even after those months in Caged, he somehow managed to ingrain himself in my soul.

The love I feel for him is something otherworldly. He's given me my life back, and all I want is to finally be happy, have a family, and perhaps even focus on a future.

"Miss Paige," one of the girls calls to me, and I realize I've been lost in my thoughts. I look up to find them all watching me.

"Sorry, girls. Let's get this routine down so you'll be ready for the dance competition coming up." Pushing off the chair, I stride to the front of the room and we lay down the steps. This is me in my element. Always. Since I was a young girl, I loved dancing, music, and learning new moves.

Being the daughter of a prestigious family, I was expected to do all the extra-curricular activities my mother dictated. Dance was one of them. At first, I thought I'd hate it. But the day that I walked into my first dance class, was the first time I felt like myself. At ease with who I was. The music, the movement of the body was something I soon became addicted to. I danced well into my late teens. Before I was taken. Shaking my head of that memory, I focus on my class and the girls I'm teaching.

They bring me happiness. So does the man I love. I'm finally who I wanted to be all those years ago. I have a family, friends, and I can be the Paige I remember.

SEVENTEEN

Kael

AFTER WHAT AXEL SAID ABOUT HARKIN BEING ALIVE, I'VE done some digging and he's right, there's no death certificate. I've tried calling Sam, but Freya said he's gone with Dax dealing with the new nightclub they're opening.

Since he should be back tonight, I'm going to get to the bottom of this. My mind is running a million miles a minute, so I don't hear her soft footfalls enter the space until she's right behind me.

"Hey, handsome," my firebird says as she pads up to me and wraps her arms around my neck. "I was thinking..." she tapers off, and I turn to regard her fully.

"Okay?" I regard her with curiosity.

"Let's go to New York for the weekend. I don't have classes tomorrow, and you're not starting your new contract till Monday." I was waiting for this, but the commission I've just been given will keep me here in Chicago for at least another three months, which will take us to Thanksgiving.

"Maybe we can go for the holidays?" I suggest, and her expression falls for a moment before she ponders the idea. Placing my index finger under her chin, I tilt her head up so those gemstone eyes meet mine. "Besides, we have missed time to catch up on."

"Christmas it is then." She smiles, settling beside me on the sofa. "I think we should look at visiting Sam and Freya as well. Perhaps we can surprise Theia and Dax," she continues talking, planning in her head.

"Sounds good. I think we can set up a family dinner. We've not had all the Wolfe kids in one home for years. Come here." Pulling her into my lap, she settles into my arms like she's been made to fit there.

Her body curls into me, and I swear to God, she purrs. "See that was exactly what I was thinking. A reunion of sorts. As long as you and Samael can be civil to each other," she smiles. Her fingers trace the ink that adorns my skin, trailing soft circles and lines over the patterns. "Let's do something now? You're not busy."

"Like?" I quiz her, inhaling the sweet scent of her perfume.

"Let's go to the lake and get a small boat or something. Or... I don't know." A pout from her beautiful lips is enough to have me lifting her in my arms and stalking toward the bedroom.

"I know what you need, Firebird. You need to fly." Setting her down, I gaze into those deep emerald eyes and cup her face in my hands. "Get dressed, but I want you bare underneath." With a soft kiss, I leave her to get ready while I pull out my phone and tap out a message to a friend I know can help me with what I need. I've made some connections in Chicago since moving here, and what I have in mind will be perfect if he agrees.

I don't have to wait long for the response I want. He's working today and he's happy to assist with my request. Shoving my phone back into my pocket, I head into the living room.

Moments later, she comes bounding into the living room dressed in a pair of jean shorts and the Phoenix tank top I made for her. With my art selling so well, I've branched out and created a line of clothing for her dance classes. The small firebird logo is branded on them with her company name—Risen from the Ashes.

"I'm ready!" she announces playfully, a smile wide on her beautiful face as she regards me shyly. I love her submissiveness, but I also love her fire. When she allows me to care for her, I'm happiest, but when I see her fly, it fills my heart. As if both parts of her make me whole.

"Let's go." I grab the keys to the Jeep, and we head out to the garage. I open the passenger door for her and she slips in without another question. The sky is clear, and I'm looking forward to seeing her reaction to what I have planned. I had to make a couple of phone calls, and luckily, my friend was working today, or this would have all gone to shit.

Once I'm inside the car, she turns to me with that inquisitive gaze, but I don't glance at her. Instead, I start the engine and pull out onto the road. It's almost midday, and the streets are busy with lunchtime traffic. Instead of heading into the town center, I turn toward the Observation Deck. It's one of the most beautiful places in the city because of the views. A small smile plays on my lips and the anticipation has my heart rate skyrocketing.

"Are you going to ignore me the whole time?" she quips and her full lips look good enough to eat with that shimmery lip gloss she loves to wear. When I finally cut a quick peek at her, I chuckle. Her bottom lip is pushed out into the sexiest little pout I've ever seen.

"Not all the time, Phoenix. Soon you'll be begging me to ignore you." With a wink, I turn into the parking lot and turn off the engine.

"We're sightseeing?" She peers out the window up at the skyscraper. I ignore her once again, and I know she's going to be fuming, which is exactly how I want her. We head through the entrance and out toward the elevator that will take us up to the deck. As we step into the empty car, I grip her hips and tug her against me, her back to my front. Her body immediately nestles where I need her, at my crotch. Her delectable ass wiggles, and I know she's doing it to taunt me. If only she knew what I have in store for her.

"This is a surprise, sweetheart, so I need you to stop pushing your sexy little ass against my cock or you'll get fucked before we reach our destination," I murmur in her ear, reveling in the shudder that runs through her. She doesn't have time to respond because we reach the deck, and Miles steps up to greet me. I shake his hand and offer a smile. "Good to see you, man."

"Glad I could help," he responds, ushering us into the space I've booked. It's not large, so I've asked him to keep it empty until we arrive, so I can get the spot I want. He exits with a grin and a shake of his head. I haven't told him what I have planned, but with my girl right up against me, I'm sure he can figure it out.

Once we're alone, I walk her over to the window overlooking the city. With this view, you can see for miles, and I know it will be one experience she'll never forget.

"This is gorgeous, Kael, but I don't understand." She pivots in my arms and peers up at me. Her long red hair flowing behind her like a river of fire.

"Turn and look out the window. What do you see?" Her gaze rakes over the view and she's silent for a while. Not long after we've gotten into position, the elevator opens and a few tourists enter behind us. We're in the corner, looking out at Lake Michigan, and I know she's concentrating on the buildings in the distance and the water that glistens under the sunlight.

Even though she's silent, I can feel the tension and anticipation radiating off her. That's when I know it's time. "Tell me, Phoenix?" I whisper in her ear, eliciting another shiver through her small frame.

"Well, just the—" Her words are halted when I tease my way down her belly. My fingertips skirting over the material of her top. When I reach my destination, her body stills and her breathing quickens. Her chest rising and falling. My two digits find their way between her legs, and I stroke her slick heat. "Kael." My name falls in a hiss from her lips. The people beside us don't notice her trembling hand as she grips the barrier, her knuckles turning white.

I'm aware of the people now filing into the area from the elevators. The small group of tourists is too interested in the view to bother with the two of us. And that is exactly why I chose this place to tease my little bird.

"Yes, baby? I thought you wanted to soar." I whisper my lips over the shell of her ear then, grazing the lobe with my teeth, biting gently while I tease her clit. "You'll be quiet, won't you? I mean, you don't want everyone to know you're about to come all over my fingers. Do you?" The question sends her spiraling, and I immediately dip two fingers into her pussy, relishing the tightness around my fingers.

"Kael, I... I..." Her words are a whisper. The pulse of her body is the only evidence she's about to unravel in public with my fingers inside her.

"That's my Firebird. Soar for me, baby. Fly and explode," I coax, cooing in her ear, and she does. Obeying me, she finds her release and soaks my hand with the sticky sweetness I'm about to savor from each digit. I wait a while until her body is still before I pull my fingers away from her heat.

Her scent is sweet—intoxicating—and I bring my fingers to her lips.

"Taste it, baby." Her tongue flicks out, licking her arousal, and I turn her around, not caring that there are people around us and crash my mouth on hers. Our lips mold together as our teeth clash and tongues fight for more, for dominance, but I win. I always do because she submits, allowing me to devour her.

I own her. Her body. Her heart. Her soul. Our kiss deepens, and I want to climb inside her. I want to be the only thing she thinks about, morning, noon, and night. I want her to ache when I'm not around, like I do when she's at work.

Before I get carried away, I break the kiss and take in her swollen lips. She's beautiful. Her cheeks are flushed and her eyes are shining with desire, with the need to have me fill her up. "I'm taking you home now," I vow. Because the only thing I can think about is fucking her until she can't move.

Owned By You

Destiny brought me you,
Life ripped us apart,
But fate had other plans,
Now our forever is a promise,
Let's walk this path together.

EIGHTEEN

Paige

I HAVE A FEW QUIET WEEKS WITH THE DANCE SCHOOL closed and I'm taking the time to catch up on my studies and the mounds of paperwork that seem to have piled themselves high on my desk. "Baby." Kael's low tone drags me from the email I'm typing out, and when I glance up, I can't help but blush at the beauty of the man who owns me.

I'm a fortunate girl, I know that, and I thank my lucky stars every day that we found each other again. That I finally have a life I want. "You ready for dinner?" I glance at the clock and realize it's already five.

"We could get take-out?" he suggests, and I nod. "Thai?" Nodding again, I hit send and rise from the chair. When I round my desk, he stalks toward me and tugs me into his arms. Leaning in, he brushes my lips with this. "One day, I'm going to marry you," he whispers and my heart leaps into my throat.

"That's some light pre-dinner conversation, Kael," I say and he presses his lips to mine. They're warm and taste like candy, and

I know he's been eating the chocolate I bought for his birthday.

"I just wanted you to know. I love you. I've always loved you. And every day I fall harder and deeper in love with you. I can't see my life without you."

Glancing into those dark eyes, I can't help but melt at his beautiful words. "I love you too, but what's got you so emotional?" I reach up, stroking his face gently. The scruff of his beard tickles my hand and I revel in the sensation, knowing how amazing it feels when his face is between my thighs.

"I just needed you to know. Sometimes we get busy with life, and things can fall between the cracks. There are times I'm romantic, you know," he quips playfully, and I nod through a smile.

"Oh, I know that, Sir." He chuckles, planting a soft kiss on my forehead, leaving me to work. Sitting back down, I start my work on the dance school plans for the new year. We want to expand and I need to apply for planning permission. The phone ringing on my desk startles me from the report I'm typing up. Swiping my thumb over the screen, I answer absentmindedly. "Hello?"

"Phoenix." Her voice is low, almost a whisper, but there's something else. She's been crying.

"What happened, Kota?" Silence greets me, and I wonder if the line cut, but when I glance at my phone, I notice I'm still connected. "Babe? Talk to me."

"I'm... Something happened with Axe. There's been calls

to his phone, nights where he doesn't come home. I'm not sure what he's doing. I have asked him about it, but he brushes it off. As if I'm being stupid for even asking," she hisses into the phone, and I wonder if Axel is home right now.

"Do you want me to call you back later?"

"No. Would you be able to take a trip out? I know you're busy with school and work, but... Do you think Kael will let you come to New York?" We'd just spoken about going for the holidays, but if Kota needs me, I'll drop everything for her.

"I'll ask. I don't think it will be a problem, babe. He knows I'd do anything for you. Hold on, let me ask him." Dropping my phone on the bed, I race to the office where Kael is busy working. I burst through the door, seizing his attention immediately. "Babe, I need a huge favor," I say, my panic palpable.

"Anything for you, Firebird." He casts a quick glance at his laptop, hits the Enter key, and drags his gaze back to me. When he takes in my expression, his face falls. "What's wrong?"

"Dakota needs me. She's on the phone right now and she's upset. Axel's been.... Well, we don't really know what happened, but I'm worried about her. He's been working long hours, he's been distant... It doesn't sound like him, and I know something's up. I just feel like I need to be there for her," I implore him, hoping he'll allow me to go to her. The understanding in his expression is enough to calm my racing heart.

He rises from his office chair and grips my shoulders, pulling me against him. "Then you'll go to her, Phoenix," he responds calmly and releases me. Turning to the desk, he opens a web browser and, seconds later, he's pulling out a credit card and booking a flight.

"Are you sure? I mean, you can come with if you want to." My concern is unwarranted, but I know what he's like. He never lets me out of his sight except for when I'm at the studio teaching. Other than that, this man commands my attention.

His dark eyes pin me, while his mouth forms a small smile. "Baby, I wouldn't let you go if I didn't trust you. I love you and I know you love Dakota. So go to her. She needs you." He tugs me forward and settles me on his lap, planting a soft kiss on my lips and I can't help smiling. This man is incredible. There are still times I wonder how I got so lucky.

"Thank you. Did I ever tell you you're amazing?" I quip playfully, and his lids drop as he stares at me with a hooded gaze.

"You can show me later." With a swift swat on my ass, he lets me go tell Dakota the good news. I bound back into the bedroom and inform my best friend and sister I'll be seeing her soon.

Once I hang up, I grab a small suitcase from the closet and drop it on the bed. I don't know how long I'll be there. Kael finds me staring at the empty bag. "You okay, baby?" He circles his strong arms around my waist and pulls me against him.

"Yeah." I nod. As soon as I heard the soft voice of my Kota, I knew something was up. Needless to say, since she told me the story, my body has been vibrating with anger and ultimately fear. She'll be crushed if he leaves. Her confidence has always been a problem for her, and now that he's acting like an asshole, I'm not sure she'll be able to take the knock if he is cheating.

Axel may be an alpha male, but he'll be answering to a strong-willed woman who takes no prisoners if he hurts her. He better come up with a fucking solid explanation, or I'll be tying him to the bedpost and whipping him.

"Phoenix." The deep rumble of my man comes from behind me. "Are you okay?"

"Yeah, I'm just worried about her. If your friend hurts her, he'll be in a world of hurt." Turning in his arms, I twine my arms around his neck. The smirk that lifts one side of his face makes me smile.

"I'm sure, baby. Somehow, I don't think he's cheating. Whatever it is, it must be for a good reason. I know my best friend, and as much as he loves women, he's not a playboy. He'd never do that to her." His words offer some comfort, but deep down, the worry still niggles at me.

Then what could he be doing?

NINETEEN

Kael

Sitting back, I sip the beer I've been nursing since I spoke to my woman. The house is quiet without her here, and I miss her. The contract I've been commissioned for is complete, and I can take time off before starting the next one.

I'm about to turn on the TV when my phone rings. Thinking it's Paige calling back, I answer quickly, expecting her melodic voice. Instead, I'm met with a response from the man I'd walked out on so many years ago. "Brother."

I've been expecting him to call with news about Harkin. We've only spoken a few times since I helped Sam get Freya out of Caged. He met her the year after Paige was freed and she was there for years before he finally called me. I don't know if it was his need to keep her close, or if he was too proud to ask for my help, but he finally came to his senses.

Before I found Paige, I swallowed the anger of the past and helped free the woman my brother loves. Not long after, I walked into Inferno and saw the redhead who held my heart.

"I hope you have news for me, Sam." I respond. My brother and I never had an easy relationship. You could call it prickly. But I've seen the change in him. And no matter what, he's my brother. The only one I have. And if my uncle is still alive, then we need to make sure that he's either put away for life, or we can teach him a lesson in torture ourselves.

Paige is convinced we need to put our dark history where it should stay. In the past.

"I do have news, it involves Paige," he responds. When he mentions my girl's name, my body goes rigid.

"What is it, Samael?" I question warily. Setting the bottle down, I push off the sofa and stalk over to the window, shoving a hand in my jeans, trying to keep from smashing the glass. The city below shimmers in the dark as I listen to him take a deep breath.

"It's about what happened to her before I took over. That night, after you left, I had to take her to Dad, but there was another man in the room I didn't know would be there." He's silent as if gathering the words, or his thoughts, I'm not sure what, but then he utters the name. "Harkin Wolfe." Even though we suspected, I forced myself not to believe it. *My uncle?*

"You mean our dead uncle?" I ask incredulously. Shaking my head, I rake my fingers through my hair and watch the lights below flicker on and off.

"He's alive. We have footage of him. Kael, I found recordings after they closed Caged and there's one of Paige. I think you need to come here and we need to make this fucker pay for what he did. My PI is on the case. He's got a lead and I'm sure by the—"

"You do realize this is us chasing a ghost?"

"He's no ghost. I'll send you the intel I have. If you feel it warrants a visit, then it's your choice, but I'm going after him." He sounds adamant. One thing about Samael is that he never takes no for an answer, and when he's got his mind set on something, nothing will stop him.

"Send it over. Paige is in New York, so I might be able to get away for a few days. Only if I feel that you're right. You may have saved her, but I haven't forgotten that you touched her."

"Look, I know we've not had the easiest relationship, but I need you to trust me. Even if it's only this one time. I'm not our father, and I certainly am not our uncle. My life is...full. I've got a woman I love, and I have my kids. I don't need this asshole coming back to cause trouble. Yes, I did take over as Paige's trainer when you left, but only because you asked me to. It was the safest thing for her and you know it."

He's got a point, so I nod in agreement, even though he can't see me. As much as I was angry for what my brother did, I can't deny that he's right, and as much as it hurts knowing he was with her, I'd trust him more than any of the other men my father had working for him. "Fine, send what you have. I'll pack a bag."

"Thank you, brother." With that, we hang up, and I realize

I'm about to spend more time with him than I have in almost ten years. I'm not sure what to expect. He's a father now, a married man. Paige told me to give our relationship as brothers a chance, and as much as I know she's right, it's a difficult thing for me to do.

Heading into the bedroom, I pull the rucksack from the closet and fill it with what I'd need for a few days away. I'm about to message Paige when an email comes through from Sam. Pulling it up, I find the information he has and it seems the filth I call uncle is alive.

Without a second thought, I pull up my contacts and send a quick message to my girl. I can't explain what I'm about to do because, honestly, I don't know what we're going to find when we finally come face to face with Harkin. My uncle is known for every illegal deed in the book, and I don't doubt he'll be wanting a fight. And if that's what he wants, I know the Wolfe brothers will give it to him.

Tapping out another message, this time to Sam, I tell him I'm on my way. If what my brother found is as bad as he says it is, I'm about to rip into the old man and make sure he never sees the light of day again. Pulling up the number for the airline, I hit Send, and as soon as my call is answered, I book a flight.

Once I've finalized my ticket, I head out the door with one thing on my mind. Watching the asshole bleed, killing him and making sure he doesn't hurt anyone again.

TWENTY

Paige

As soon as the plane touched down, I rushed home wondering where Kael's been because I haven't received the morning call I got every day since I've been with Kota, which is unusual. He sent me a text saying that there's a contract he's busy with, but other than that he's not called. He's so protective and all consuming. For him not to reach out is strange. As I push tentatively through the front door and step inside, I'm met with the deafening silence of an empty house.

A week is a long time away from him and I'm sure he's feeling it too. I miss him. "Kael?" Silence greets me. It's an eerie sound in the large living space. "Babe?" Once again my voice echoes and calls to an empty house. An icy chill of fear runs deep in my veins, and I wonder if something's happened. The thought niggles in my mind, and even though I was ready to come home sooner, I didn't let Dakota know I was worried about him.

I was torn. She needed me, and I needed him. But after everything we've been through, I figured he was just busy with his contract. There are times when he hides in his studio, and I get that, but this feels different. Something is off. As soon as I pad into our bedroom—and find it empty—doubt slowly seeps into my mind.

Doubt about us. About him.

It's stupid, I know this, but I've always had this weakness when it comes to him. The memories of the last time he walked out slam into me full force, leaving me breathless and afraid. My blood chills, wondering if someone from our past has caught up to us. Perhaps one of my old clients. Or maybe...my father? No. It can't be. Would he do something to Kael? I haven't seen him or tried to contact him or my mother since I was freed. After learning what he did, I wished he were dead. Perhaps that's not good, but I couldn't help myself. My anger at the man I loved for eighteen years of my life is overwhelming.

Racing back into the kitchen, I pull out my phone and hit dial on his number. After two rings, it goes to voice mail. When I tap the call button again, I'm met with the same automated message that he's not available and to leave a message. My mind duels with possibilities of what could have happened to him. Of him packing and leaving, which doesn't make sense. Things were good between us. At least, they were the last time we spoke, which was yesterday morning. Almost twenty-four hours have passed and all I have is a text message.

My body wracks with a sob so harsh and so deep, I feel it in my bones and collapse on the tiles.

He's left. He must have.

Why would he be avoiding my calls?

I try his phone again—this time it goes directly to voicemail. Not a ring, not a beep, nothing. Just silence.

It doesn't make sense. He wouldn't just walk out on us. *Could he?* I'm tempted to call Dakota, but she and Axel are working through their own hurdles. For the first time in a long time, I'm truly alone. I've spent years depending on myself, but once I got used to having Kael back, I let my independence slip just a little, and now he's gone and I feel as if I'm lost.

I push up from the floor and head into the bedroom. Pulling open the closets, I find his black duffle gone. There are jeans and shirts in messy piles, which is unlike him. As if he packed in a hurry.

I head toward the bed and flop onto it. Thoughts of him leaving me poison my mind. Images of him walking away make breathing difficult. Maybe he realized he was better off without me while I was away. Or there's someone else. Someone better. *Did I even mean anything to him?*

Doubt is a bitch. She strolls in with confidence oozing from every pore. Gripping you by the heart and seducing your mind with negativity so deep-rooted it blackens your soul. And as I lie there in the darkening room, I find her my best friend. The last time I lost Kael it *almost* killed me. This time, though, I think it will succeed.

Tears sting my eyes. The salty wetness flows like an emotional waterfall down my heated cheeks. The ache in my heart is unlike anything I've ever felt. It steals my breath. It shakes me to the very core of my being. It's as if the silence is mocking me, taunting me, telling me how unworthy I am of a man like him. All those years ago he walked out without so much as a backward glance. I know it wasn't his fault, but in the confusion swirling through my mind, it feels as if he's done it again.

Granted, the last time was because of his father. But this time it's on him.

Pushing off the bed, I let my anger and fear get the better of me. I head straight for the liquor cabinet and find the man I'm looking for. It's childish. I should call Kota and Axel, but right now, all I want to do is wallow. I want to cry. My heart hurts, as if it's been ripped from my chest and sliced open, bleeding my emotion onto the floor at my feet.

Grabbing the bourbon, I murmur, "Hello, Jack." I grin at the bottle and crack the lid. He couldn't even leave me a fucking note. A Dear John letter. There's just nothing.

Padding over to the kitchen, I find the small shot glasses Dakota bought me for my birthday. When I read the message on the side, I can't help giggling through the tears. *Smile if you swallow.* "Yes, Kitten, I do indeed. Mr. Jack will be my man tonight." Once I've gotten what I need—glass, bottle, tissues—I flop onto the sofa and down shot after shot. I swallow them all, and along with each burning gulp, the anger and frustration and all the years of pain without the man I love, make their way into my bloodstream.

"Phoenix." A soft whisper at my left ear rouses me from a dreamless sleep, or I may have passed out. I'm not sure. "Paige, baby." The voice is louder now. It's right inside my head, drumming at the inside of my eyes, and it hurts.

Throb. Bang. Throb. *Shit.*

"Jesus, baby, how much did you drink?" A sweet smell hits me right in the gut, and the alcohol I'd consumed the night before swirls like a tornado in my stomach. A shiver wracks my body, and I'm suddenly freezing. Water running alerts me that I'm no longer on the sofa, but in the bathroom.

When I dare crack my eyes, I find Kael staring back at me. Concern etched on his perfect face. "Kael?" The word feels foreign, and I'm certain I'm dreaming. I'm lost to the agony that engulfed me last night. "You're real?" His touch is warm, searing my skin.

"I am, baby. Why the hell did you finish a bottle of bourbon on your own?" he questions, confusion furrowing his brows in earnest. A second wave of nausea hits me. I push him away, falling to my knees at the porcelain bowl. My body convulses painfully. My hair is tugged back, but I swat his hand away.

The shower is still running, but I don't care about that as the pain morphs into anger. "Fuck you. Get away from me." His body stills beside me, and confusion mixed with anger swarms around him. *I've spoken out of turn.* He was the one who left without so much as a fucking note, and now suddenly he's trying to be caring.

Arms encircle me, and once again, the whiff of sweetness fills my nostrils. *His shirt.* It's coming from Kael, and more anger hits me, punches me so hard my body convulses with a cry, a sob, a fucking painful reminder that he left and now that he's back, he smells of someone else.

"What the fuck is wrong with you, Phoenix?" he bites out in frustration, and I meet his dark glare.

"I said, get the hell away from me. If I have to smell someone else on you, I'll rip your fucking balls off!" I hiss in anger. Instead of the angry retort I expect him to blast me with, he chuckles. The sound feels foreign in my mind. He shouldn't be laughing. How can he do this to me? He was with someone else and now he's laughing at me? Rage consumes me, and I see red. Fisting my hands, I plough them into his solid chest, and he allows it. Only two punches with each hand before he grips my wrists so hard, I yelp.

"Stop. Stop it now or I will tie you up and fuck you raw," he grunts and tugs me over to him. My legs automatically straddle him. His gaze burns into me, boring a hole right through my gaping chest. "I wasn't with another woman last night, baby. Well, not in the way you think," he murmurs, burying his nose in my neck and inhaling my scent. "You smell. Let's get you showered."

"I'm not going anywhere until you tell me why you smell like perfume. And it's not mine," I bite back, ripping my hands from his. I scramble off him and rise to full height.

When he finally stands up, he rakes his fingers over the beard he's been growing. "I was with Samael and Freya. I probably smell like Layla, their daughter."

"Oh." My anger slowly dissipates, and my glower softens into a sheepish stare.

"Jesus, you're a little firecracker. Aren't you, baby?"

"Why weren't you answering any of my calls?" Peeking up at him through my lashes, I meet those dark eyes. He watches me for a moment before sighing. He knows I'm stubborn, there's no way he's going to get away from an explanation right here, right now.

"I was doing something..." His words taper off and I watch something flicker behind his expression. "Illegal. I needed to focus so I turned my phone off."

"Illegal?" I squeak, causing the throb in my mind to return with a vengeance. "What? I mean. You were with Sam?" He nods.

"I'll explain once you've showered and you're awake. Please baby, it's important." This time he implores me, and I relent. I nod and he offers an ominous smirk. "But, let me tell you something." He pulls away, meeting my emerald gaze. "If you ever think I'm cheating on you, I'll spank your ass so fucking red that you'll not be able to move for at least a month. I don't want anyone else, you're mine. You're my forever. My love, my life, my heart. Do you understand me?"

"Yes, I just—"

He interrupts me by placing a finger on my lips, silencing my words. "There's nothing else to say on this matter. Tonight I'll punish you accordingly, because you've got me hard as fuck and I can't do it now. We need to talk." His face falls, and I realize this must be serious.

"What is it about?"

"Get in the shower. I'll be right back." He leaves me in the steamy bathroom, and I shed my clothes which smell of puke and bourbon. My stomach roils at the stench, and I quickly deposit the offending items in the laundry hamper.

Stepping under the spray, I allow it to wash the sadness from my mind and the ache from my heart.

He didn't leave me.

How could I have even thought that?

Because he's done it before. I realize the agony from the first time I lost him has propelled a fear of abandonment that he'll do it again.

As much as he's promised me forever, sometimes that bitch

called doubt steps in and tangles her claws in my mind.

"Get out of your head, Firebird," he growls from behind me. I spin on my heel to find Kael in all his naked glory. His body is perfect, with a smattering of dark chest hair, which gives him a manly look that leaves my thighs clenching.

"I'm..."

"Turn around, face the wall and bend at the waist." His command is strong and harsh, but the slight growl that rumbles in his chest tells me he's ready to mark me. And I so want him to do that. To make me ache and scream. For him to show me how much he owns me.

I wait for the slap or the tip of his cock to tease me, but it's only when I feel a finger at my puckered hole do I gasp. "What—"

"Teaching you a lesson in respecting your Master," he tells me easily. I can hear the smirk in his tone. I've fucked up I know that, and he's going to enjoy punishing me. "Place your hands on the tiles and hold on, baby," he murmurs as he slowly teases a finger into me.

The sensation of him fingering my ass is too much causing me to mewl loudly. The sound bounces off the tiles and through the cascading spray, I revel in the sensations racing through me.

Another finger joins the first and as he scissors me open, my legs begin to tremble. I've never had an orgasm from anal alone, but the way Kael is taunting me, I'm sure it will happen. But, as suddenly as it started, he pulls both fingers from me and replaces them with something cold.

"Just breathe, relax." We've played with toys before, but this feels bigger, thicker. The metal plug slips past the tight ring and I'm immediately filled to the max.

"God..." A moan falls from my lips.

"That's Sir to you, Phoenix." He chuckles and rains a harsh slap on each cheek. My body quivers, and I instinctively push back against his crotch. A feather light touch strokes my bare lips and circles my clit. An orgasm taunts me, tightening everything below my belly button, but as soon as I grasp the feeling, his fingers leave me wanting, panting, and aching. "Let's see how long you can last."

With that, he steps out of the shower and grabs a towel, wrapping it around his waist.

"But—" I rise to find myself alone and needy. Torture. He's torturing me.

Jesus, I'm in for a long day.

TWENTY ONE

Kael

THOUGHTS OF THE LAST COUPLE OF DAYS ARE RUNNING rampant in my mind. It took us time, but we found the asshole, now I need to talk to Paige about him.

Once the cab pulls up to Sam and Freya's home, I pay and exit the vehicle. As soon as I reach the door and knock it swings open and I'm met with cobalt eyes. He holds out a hand. "Kael, I'm glad you came. I didn't want to do this alone."

"Anything for my girl," I offer a smile, shaking my brother's hand in camaraderie. "It's good to see you." He steps aside, allowing me inside his home. I've never been here and I take a moment to flit my gaze over it.

It's so homely. Warm and inviting. We head into the living room and I'm assaulted by the scent of freshly brewed coffee. Freya enters with a beautiful smile. "Kael, so good to see you," she wraps her arms around me, and I can't help hugging her close.

"I'm sorry it's not under better circumstances," I say. She nods, stepping back to look at her husband.

"I'll leave you two. Goodnight Kael." With a kiss for her husband, we're left alone with piles of folders and files, as well as a large pot of caffeine.

"I'm sure the kids will be happy to see you." Something in that moment makes me want to apologize. I'm not sure what for, but we both settle on the sofa before I speak.

"Look, Sam. This was never an easy thing for me. You took to life with Harlan like it was your destiny. I wasn't built that way. I wanted love, a family."

"I know. I never blamed you. Yeah, I was pissed when you left, when he threw you out, but that night something in me snapped. I couldn't be in that house alone. You were always the one who I knew would make it out. There's something I need to confess. When I met Freya, I knew it was time I got out. When I stopped being selfish and broke her out, something happened." He's silent for a long while, but then he meets my gaze. "I haven't told Theia yet, but, one night Dad made me watch a recording of what he did to my woman, I lost it in that moment. I guess all my anger and rage from the years of abuse at his hand finally got to me. Dax didn't kill dad, I did."

Shock slams into me. I open my mouth to respond, but I can't find the words.

"Dax was there, he helped me cover it up. Thing is, because the FBI was involved I didn't want to implicate you or little Wolfe." He uses Theia's nickname I gave her when we were teens. "I choked him. I watched the light in his eyes flicker out like a flame and I didn't care. The remorse I felt was because I didn't do it sooner. And taking a life, even one as evil as his, was difficult."

"Sam, we're family. You should have come to us. We're blood. No matter what the fuck happens." A connection I've never felt with Sam is there between us in this moment. A sense of kinship. Friendship. Brothers.

"I need to figure out how to tell Theia I killed our father," he says quietly.

"We will. Let's sort Harkin out and we'll talk to little Wolfe together." He nods, and we spend the next few hours going through the documents. By three in the morning, I'm exhausted, but I look at him and ask for the main reason I'm here. "Can I see the recording of Paige?"

"It's hard to watch," he warns before popping open the laptop and inserting a portable drive into the slot. He clicks on the one titled "Paige" and when the screen fills with a scene playing out, I'm ready to rip someone to shreds.

My blood simmers, then reaches boiling point as anger and rage race through my veins while I watch what they did to my girl. My vision blurs, all I see is red. The need for revenge runs rife, choking me with emotion I can't explain. "We need to find this fucker, I want to watch him bleed. Prison is too good for him. He needs to fucking burn."

"I agree. We'll find him, Kael. I promise you brother." And just like that, the two Wolfe brothers have joined forces to bring down the last remaining filth in our family.

Finding my uncle was luck, but when I finally laid my eyes on him, I wanted to watch him bleed to death. Fury made me slam my fist into him until he was a bleeding mess. Sam pulled me off and told me we needed the girls to decide his fate. He's right. I needed to talk to Paige first. Both Freya and Paige need to put their past behind them.

I'll tell her I saw the recording of what he did to her. Just thinking about it makes me want to murder. To slice him to shreds and bathe in his blood. *Jesus, get a hold of yourself.*

We've got a plan, though. He's gone to talk to Freya, and I'm going to talk to Paige. They're the ones who need to decide what they want to do. If they want revenge, we will most certainly stand by and support them. But, if they want us to do it, I'm ready. I've been ready for a long time.

When Sam told me he killed our father, first shock hit me, but then relief. What kind of son would feel relief hearing his brother killed their father? Me. And guilt was nowhere to be found because that piece of shit deserved it. Fuck, he should have been maimed and tortured.

Paige pads barefoot into the kitchen, and I can tell she's uncomfortable. Her body is craving release. I can tell by the shimmer in her eyes—they're alight with desire. But, before I get to play, we need to talk. Let's see how she handles that butt plug in her cute ass while we have a relaxing conversation about what the fuck she was thinking getting piss-ass drunk while I was sorting out shit with my brother.

"Why do I have to wear a butt plug?" She pouts as she settles on the stool. Her actions are slow and I can't help grinning. With each movement, her body will feel the heaviness of the plug which will taunt her. Today she'll learn to never fucking doubt me or my love for her. Ever.

"Because you're being punished. Can you tell me why I feel the need to do that?" I question. She stares at me. I can see the wheels turning in her pretty little head. The petulance dances in her eyes. She wants to retort, but she should know better and she does.

"I was stupid to think you'd leave me," she mumbles. *Good girl.*

"Yes, for being bad, for jumping to conclusions, and for not trusting my love for you," I inform her while placing a mug of coffee before her. She gratefully lifts the steamy cup to her lips, and I watch as she savors the liquid.

"But—"

"No buts, unless it's yours," I interrupt, offering her a smirk. Swallowing the last of my coffee, I regard her earnestly. "I needed to talk to you about something, though. It might bring back memories." My voice drops, and I watch her reaction. "Bad ones."

"Kael, I'm a big girl. What's wrong?"

Inhaling a deep breath, I reach for her hand, and when she slips mine in hers, I start my story. "I left two days ago to see Samael. He called me and told me that my uncle was still alive." Lifting her hand, I plant a soft, chaste kiss on her knuckles. "When Caged closed down, Sam found some recordings of the girls, he showed me one of you, from the day after I left..."

I allow my words to taper off, hoping she'll be honest and tell me the horrors she faced. I've seen it, every minute, each moment of her debasement. The depraved things he did to her in those parties. Six men to one girl. All the recordings were the same, each girl went through the same vile ordeal.

"If you've seen it, why do I need to tell you what happened?" She pulls her hand from my grip and rises from the stool. Her body shivers with what I can only guess is fear. Of course she doesn't want to recall those horrific things, but I need her words to fuel her.

I need her angry, so when I tell her that we've got the fucker holed up in the basement of his house, she'll be ready to do what needs to be done. For her to get the revenge that she deserves. I also want her rabid, because I need to fuck the anger out of me and into her.

The craving to take her and climb inside her, just so I can hold her soul while she screams my name when she comes undone, is vicious.

"When you left, Sam came to my room the next morning. He told me he'd be training me since you'd been told to leave," she starts.

Her voice is a million miles away, and I wonder if she's walking back through time. If she's in that room at this moment.

"He allowed me to dress, then he walked me to this room, bound me and left me there to be hurt by your father, even though he was in a mask I recognized his voice. There was another man though. I didn't know him, he also wore a mask. There's something not on those recordings though. There were other times where a man would collect me. One who wasn't Sam. He used to take me to a part of the mansion none of the other girls knew about. I'd asked them. The man who ran these parties wasn't your father, at least I didn't see him there. This man who was hurting me wasn't him because his voice was different." She falls silent and I'm certain this is my father's wing, which Samael had mentioned. Growing up, I don't remember ever knowing about this section of the house.

"And then what happened?"

She turns to me then, her green gaze pinned on my brown ones. "There were these parties. Six men, always six," she murmurs as if saying it softly will make it a bad dream. "They would..." Tears glisten in her eyes, and I make my way to her, but she holds up a hand, stopping me in my tracks. "Each man would take turns. Sometimes, there'd be more than one at a time. The worst was when they hurt me just to hear me scream. When I had two of them in one of my..." It's then that she breaks down, and I can't not hold her. Closing the distance, I grab her in my arms and plant a soft kiss on her hair.

Her sobs are otherworldly, and I regret asking her to relive it. But she needs to let this out. "That man. The one who..."—I can't say the words—"with my father. His name is Harkin Wolfe, my father's twin brother. I saw what he did to you baby, but I need you to listen to me now." I step back and cup her face in my hands. Lifting her head, I meet her stare dead on. "We found him. If you want revenge, you can have it. All you have to do is say the word and we'll go there and you can torture him as much as you want to." My words halt her tears and she's silent for a long while. Moments pass. Minutes tick by. Then she nods.

"I want to."

I nod my understanding with pride. "Then it's settled. I'll let Sam know. We'll go with you." Pulling her into my arms again, I inhale her scent. From her freshly showered skin, to the sweet scent of her shampoo. My perfect woman. "Now"—I release my hold on her and glance at her body—"this isn't the best time to do this, but I need you. I need to take all those memories and rid you of them. I'm yours, you're mine. I'm your fuel, you're my fire, and together, baby, we're going to burn the past from your mind."

"Kael." My name is a whimper, a plea, and I want nothing more than to devour her right here. Leaning in, I scoop her up, bridal style, and head up to our bedroom.

"I wanted to punish you all day for doubting me, but I can't wait. You're my one weakness, Paige Madden, and there's nothing more I want than to be with you forever." My words have her breath hitching. This is what I've wanted since the first time I laid my eyes on her. To make her Mrs. Wolfe. To bind her to me forever and watch her body swell and change as she bears my children.

"Is that your way of proposing, Kael Wolfe?" she quips. Her gaze still holds the memories she recalled, and I plan on fucking them out of her right now.

"If I was proposing, Firebird, you'd know. That was just a promise." I place her on her feet and cross my arms in front of my chest. "Take off your clothes, bend over the edge of the bed, and wait." She obeys beautifully, and I take in the soft curves of her ass with the sparkly plug sitting snug between luscious cheeks. "You look beautiful with my toys inside your body, Paige."

"Are you going to stand there and watch me, or are you going to exact your punishment? When we're done, I'd like to go and dole out my revenge." Her tone is adamant, and I've never been more in awe of this woman. She's been through hell—and that's no exaggeration—yet here she is, sassing me about wanting to kill a man. I can't help loving her even more. Every day that passes, I fall deeper, harder, and more in love with Paige.

"Oh, you'll get your punishment, and I can't wait to see you take charge and avenge yourself, baby. The thought of that makes me harder than rock," I say, lifting the long, black feather from the shelf.

"Thank you." Her words still me and she continues. "For giving me my life back." With that, I decide the punishment I had planned will suffice.

I don't respond with words, instead, I trail the feather over her spine, from her neck to her ass. Soft whimpers fall from her lips, but she doesn't move. *Good girl.* I should tell her, but I wait. Another light trail over her hip, down her thighs, I allow my hot breath to fan over her drenched core. Her scent is heavenly as I inhale the sweetness waiting for me.

Grabbing the small pinwheel, I start at the base of her spine and roll it up along her back. The sensations that this elicits have her shuddering. With my free hand, I rain a swat on her ass, harsh and loud. Her moans are like music, echoing around us. Spurring me on, I slap her cheeks, left, right, left, right, until my handprints are evident. "Do you need my cock yet, Phoenix?" I hiss as she pushes her ass back against my rigid erection.

"Please, Sir. Fuck me, please," she pleads. I know there are tears rolling down her cheeks, only this time, they're not of sadness, but instead of pure pleasure.

"Open your legs." She spreads them easily, and I kneel behind her. The silver of the pinwheel glints in the bright light streaming through the bedroom windows. With precision, I press the steel to her glistening lips and she lets out a yelp, fisting the sheets, while chanting my name, over and over again.

When I reach her clit, her cries become animalistic. I love watching her teeter on the edge. Her release just out of reach. It's how I love to taunt her.

"Are you ready now, baby?" I ask against her sex and she practically screeches my name. Rising, I push my jeans and boxer briefs to the floor and grip my now steel shaft. Teasing her lips with the crown, I inch into her, the movement is slow and I know it's torture on her body.

"God, Kael, please. Goddammit, please!" Smirking at her words, I roll my hips and slam into her, seating myself to the hilt, and the octave her screams take on must wake the dead. Her body convulses and pulses around me when I feel her soak my cock with her sweet juices.

"Did you just come without my permission, Phoenix?" I quip, and she nods. With that, my hand rains down four slaps to her ass cheeks. She must be overwhelmed. Filled to the max with the plug and my cock. I knew she'd come, but that just makes me smile, because I made her feel that good.

"I'm sorry, Sir. I just—"

I pull out and ram back into her, again and again, snuffing out the words she was about to utter as I fuck her. Gripping her hips, I hold her steady as all the anger, frustration, and memories I know she held gets ripped from her mind as I drive into her.

It's animalistic. It's violent. It's unapologetic.

It's us.

My Phoenix. My woman. My fucking pet.

Her body tightens and I know she's close. "You're going to come with me this time, baby," I bite out, my jaw clenching painfully as I try to hold on to my own release until I know she's ready. When my hips buck wildly and she pushes her ass against me, I realize she's there. I reach for the plug, and as I command her release, I pull it from her body as I plunge into her sweet, tight, cunt. "Now."

One word and our world tilts, her body tightens, my mind blanks out and everything around us explodes. We both detonate like a comet exploding in the sky as it reaches maximum speed.

Her cries, my grunts, everything thrums as I empty myself deep inside her. Filling not only her body, but her heart. And in that moment, I bind our souls, for the rest of eternity.

TWENTY TWO

Paige

"ARE YOU SURE YOU'RE READY FOR THIS?" KAEL STARES AT ME with concern on his face. This is it—my final chance at moving on. To see the man who hurt me so many years ago. Who took from me. With one of the vile devils dead and buried, he's the only one left who still haunts me.

Even though I haven't told Kael, he hears me some nights when I whimper and cry, begging for them to stop. Those nights will probably always haunt me. "I'm ready. This is it, I need to do this." He nods, slipping a strong hand into mine as he pushes the thick metal door open.

As soon as I step inside, the man in question, Satan himself, is there bound to a chair. His face is bloodied—I'm sure Sam has had time with him. His eyes are covered, but I'm sure he can tell we've walked in. When Samael slices the blindfold off, dark evil eyes fall on me and I'm slammed with painful memories. When he opens his mouth, the deep rumble of his voice sends revulsion skating down my spine.

"Ah, you've brought the pretty redhead," he growls.

"Shut it." Kael's angry bark is enough to scare anyone, but I know this vile piece of shit won't be perturbed by it.

"Do you know I tasted her, Kael? I made her pretty holes bleed, and then I licked it up. I cleaned her with my tongue." His words drip venom and Kael rears back and punches the old man so hard, I hear the crack of bones below his fist.

Glancing around the room, I find what I need. A sleek silver blade glints with promise. The vow to get my closure. Stepping toward him, I lift the blade and trail it over his cheek, pressing the tip into the wrinkled skin just below his eye. When I glance up, I'm met with the steel gray eyes of my tormentor. The man who not only raped me, but hurt me almost beyond repair. I say almost, but because I'm even though I was shattered, I was broken, I'm now stronger.

"So you do remember me. You know, of all the girls you hurt, it's a wonder you remember any of them." His gaze pins me with an icy glare.

"Sweet toy, you of all the whores I fucked, had the sweetest cunt. Your blood was delicious. Like a drug, it made me so fucking hard." He sneers, and I can't stop my hand coming down slicing his face from the ear down to his lips. Blood drips from the gaping flesh and I can't help smiling. I've turned into a maniac, but I don't care. "Kael, your pet is something else." He glances at the man behind me.

Dark brown eyes pin me to the spot and a sinister smirk plays on his mouth. Suddenly the door flies open and there with her beautiful light is Freya. She steps inside and just behind her is Samael. His blue gaze meets mine and he nods.

"Ah, the little Angel. You boys have good taste in toys." Harkin flits his gaze between the four of us. Freya reaches for the knife, leans in, and gets close to his face.

"You are filth. There's nothing in this world that will make me not want to do this, because after all you've done, you deserve much worse. Perhaps we should soak you in gas and light you up. I'd love to watch you burn. To see your skin flay off your bones and see your blood pool on the floor. I'll bask in it." Her words are chilling. For a sweet-looking girl, her mind is scary.

Her hand lifts and she presses the tip below his left eye. The skin pierces and a purely animalistic scream that's utter agony roars from him. Blood drains from his eye and Freya continues her torture on the other eye. Her smile is manic. "Angel." Sam's deep rumble comes from behind me, and he steps forward. His grasp on her wrist must calm her because she stops trembling. "I'll finish this." He takes the knife and steps forward.

The old man meets his gaze and smirks. "Do you have the courage to finish it, Sammy?" He chuckles and before we know it, the man who saved my life pushes the knife into his chest and we all watch. Me with fascination. Freya in awe. Kael's arms circle around me. When Samael steps back, he leaves the blade and watches the blood drain from the monster. Crimson liquid which he wretched from me now gushes through his crisp, white button up.

I've never been a violent person. I've never thought that one day I'd watch a man die in front of me and be happy. But as I see the light dim in those steely eyes, I smile.

After the pain. After the assault. Watching this, I know I'll walk away with closure. With the knowledge that justice has been served.

Since I watched the man who hurt me die, I've been wondering how people can be so evil. All that time I spent in Caged, all those clients, men who were apparently well known, pillars of society even, with their sick, evil needs were hidden behind masks. Covering up what they were doing, they hoped their dark secrets would be kept that way, until Sam shone a light on everything.

I should be studying, but my mind has been working overtime, remembering what I did. What I witnessed. "Baby." Kael's voice startles me, and I roll over to see him dressed in his painting jeans.

They're ripped, hanging low on his hips. I take in the taut muscles and *V* line that taunts me. "You're looking amazing," I say, biting my pencil. I rake my eyes over his body, and when I reach his face, I'm met with a sinful smirk.

He steps inside the room and immediately the air shifts and hangs heavy with desire. Pushing up, I sit crossing my legs. A heated gaze drops between my thighs and fire blazes behind those dark chocolate pools.

"Is there something else on your mind, handsome?" He nods, crooking his finger and I'm immediately on my knees, my legs spread, presenting him with my body.

"Take your top off, I want to see those sweet tits," he orders, and my tank top finds a spot on the rug beside me. "So beautiful," he murmurs.

"Thank you, Sir."

"Sit back, touch your pussy, I want to watch you get wet for me." Shifting onto the floor, I spread my legs and stroke myself over the soft material of my panties. "God, Firebird, you're so beautiful."

"Sir, touch me," I whimper, shifting my thong to the side, flashing him my smooth sex. Swiftly, I'm grasped and tugged up and against his body.

"Take those fucking panties off, now." Shoving the material down my thighs, I step out of them and big hands grip my ass, lifting me, pressing against the cold wall and Kael's hands move below me. The zipper hisses in the silence, and his smooth, steel shaft nudges my entrance. "You want this?" he taunts, teasing me with the crown of his dick and I whimper. Rolling my hips, needing him to fuck me. I dig my nails into his shoulders and the growl that emanates from his chest is evidence that he's barely holding on to his restraint.

"Fuck me," I moan loudly and without warning, he impales me on his thick cock. "Yessss..." A hiss falls from my lips as he drives into me. His mouth finds my nipple and his teeth, grazing over the hardened bud, bite down and my body convulses.

"Jesus, Phoenix, your little cunt is milking my cock," he grunts, and I feel his hot seed bathing me. Marking me. Our mouths meet in a soul-searing kiss.

A long drive home is the last thing I need. My feet hurt, my body aches, and the only thing I can think about is a hot shower and a comfortable bed. Maybe I can get Kael to give me a massage. Or... Maybe we can play out a scene. Thinking about that already has me squirming in my seat. It's been two long weeks since we've really spent time with the flogger and cuffs, and I'd like to find that heightened relaxation today.

There are days I love my job more than anything, but sometimes, I just want to have a day to myself. Some peace and quiet. I suppose, when they're your own kids, there is no peace and quiet. I can't help smiling at the thought of having little versions of Kael running around. If we had girls, I could teach them to dance. Or perhaps they'd like to paint. I know he'd love that. Teaching them all he knows. Without thinking, my hand circles my belly and it flip-flops, wondering if and when we'll have our chance.

As soon as I pull into the driveway and park the car, I let a yawn fall from my lips. Exiting the car, I make my way up the stairs to the front door. Weariness has my mind running at a million miles a minute. There were too many kids, and the nonstop classes put a strain on me.

Pushing open the door, I step inside the house and find it in complete darkness. *Strange.* I know Kael's home. He sent me a message to let me know he'd arrived home from the gallery only an hour ago.

Perhaps he's busy in the studio, which means he hasn't made dinner, and that means we're getting take-out. There's no way I'm going to be cooking right now. Dropping my keys and purse on the counter, I place the gym bag on the floor.

Turning to the wall, I'm about to turn on the light, when I feel something covering the switch. My fingers run over it, but don't find purchase to tug whatever it is off. I hope he's not messing around with me again. I'm too tired for his games. The man is worse than a child.

"Kael?" I call out, but only silence greets me. Maybe he's been called back and he's working late. He generally goes in to meet with artists and photographers who want to hire the studio for a day or two. In the dim silver light of the moon streaming through the window, I manage to head into the living room without breaking a leg. Upon entering the space, I find a translucent blue light shimmering on the floor. "Babe, are you here?" I pull off my hoodie and lay it on the sofa beside me. When I crouch down, I notice the blue light is coming from plastic tubing. The tiny bulbs inside the cable glow at me in the dark.

Lifting my gaze, I notice the blue leading toward the studio which is upstairs beside the master bedroom. I rise to my feet and slowly edge my way along the trail of light, following the path toward the stairs, which will take me to the bedrooms. My heart rate increases when I find a small note attached to the wall with a blue bulb shining on it at the base of the staircase.

YOU'RE MY LIGHT IN THE DARK, FIREBIRD.

His words. His handwriting. A small smile plays on my lips, knowing he's up to something. My pulse skitters, thrumming wildly as I try to figure out what he's done. There've been times when he's planned romantic evenings with rose petals and massage oils, leaving me tiny notes to follow. I take a tentative step up and find another note not far from the first.

Before my mind can come up with possibilities, I read the next message.

YOUR FIRE BLAZES IN MY HEART FOR ETERNITY.

My stomach is in disarray as butterflies tumble around, awakening a need. My love. My desire. Everything he does only makes me love him more. If that is even possible. Dragging my gaze up, I find two more lights shining down on little notes like the first two. I rush up to the third one plucking it from the wall. The words still my heart and tears sting my eyes.

YOU'RE MY FIRST, MY LAST, AND MY FOREVER.

The words become blurry as I regard this message. These words mean more than he could ever realize. It's been a rocky road for us, but it feels as if finally, we're on the straightened path. I try to swallow down the lump of emotion in my throat. My hands are trembling as I inch my way up to the last note and lift it from the sticky tape that holds it against the wall.

SO THIS IS WHY, I NEED TO KNOW...

The words taper off. I head up to the landing and find the studio lit up in blue and red. It shimmers in the dark, and as soon as I walk into the large area, I fall to my knees and the tears tumble, rolling down my cheeks.

One bare, white wall has blue and red tubing illuminated to

create the final note.

WILL YOU MARRY ME?

I can't stop the tears, the emotions. I love him so much, more than anyone I've ever known. For five long years, I didn't know if I'd ever find love. Happiness. But he's brought it all back to me. Given me a life I never thought I'd have.

"Kael?" My gaze darts around, and when he steps out of the shadows, I see him dressed in his work jeans which hang low on his hips. His toned torso is bare, and he's holding a single red rose. The smirk on his face is enough to have me giggling. He's so proud of himself. He should be. This was a surprise. I knew he'd ask me one day, but this is one of the most romantic things he's ever done.

"Phoenix," he murmurs as he nears me. The emotion overwhelms me, tightening my chest almost painfully, but elation sweeps it away when he drops to one knee before me and hands me the flower. I notice a thin white ribbon looped through a ring, fastened with a bow on the thorn free stem.

It's beautiful, elegant, and simple. Perfect. A square cut diamond surrounded by tiny rubies set in a circle on a beautiful white gold band. "This is... this..." My gaze flits around, and I settle my attention back on the message. It glows at me, asking, pleading, imploring me, and out of all the decisions I've made in my life, this is the easiest. There's no doubt in my mind what my answer will be. It's always been one word.

"So?" he whispers urgently.

"I can't say anything but yes, Kael. I love you." I leap into his arms, and he tumbles backward. He chuckles at my excitement as I settle myself on top of him. Our mouths crash together in a soul-stealing kiss, and I know we've been bound forever, not just now, but many years ago when his lips first touched mine.

EPILOGUE

Paige

A LONG DAY HAS PASSED. WE'VE BEEN DOING SOME DIGGING into the past, mainly to gain closure on everything. I've legally changed my name. The Madden name is part of my history. I didn't want to be tied to that family anymore. Kael is my family now.

Kael said I should go to them—talk to my parents—but there's no way I would be able to look them in the eye after what they did. Giving me to a vile man like Harlan Wolfe for a seat in the senate. My father will get what's coming to him.

We've also had tests done on the DNA of Harkin and Harlan. When they ran tests on the body of Harkin Wolfe, there were questions that popped up regarding his children. We didn't realize he had any, but it seems something came up. Now we have to wait for them to trace the blood samples and find his next of kin.

Since the closure of Caged, which was later turned into a

sanctuary for battered women, there've been speculations that Harkin fathered a daughter who was in Caged. We don't know who she is yet, though.

I settle back, jotting notes for my next class. With a roaring fire, and the man I love beside me, I'm in my element. The sofa is warm, and so are Kael's arms. He's watching the television, which is—as always—on so loud, it's drowning out the sound of the music from my earphones.

I swear, the man is going deaf the older he gets. Giggling at my wayward thoughts, I pull my earphones from my ears, regarding him. His face is one of concentration as he watches the images on screen. "Babe, please turn it down. I'm working on a new routine and I can't concen—" My words are cut short when the newscaster announces the next story.

"Breaking news just in. This evening, Senator Madden was taken in along with his wife of more than thirty-years for questioning. They've been named as accomplices in the debacle that brought down the infamous nightclub Caged which was operating from a large property on the outskirts of New York. This is the same club where the prostitution ring had been holding girls and women prisoner forcing them to work in Caged.

Evidence was found in the home of Harkin Wolfe, the brother of the owner of Caged, Harlan Wolfe. Both Wolfe men were said to have bought and sold young girls into a life of sexual slavery. It seems our senator was one of the regulars of Caged, and had only secured his votes with the help of long-time business partner Harlan.

There was confirmation that the senator and his wife had also kept the disappearance of their daughter, Paige Madden, from the authorities by payments made to cover their story of her whereabouts for almost ten years. When questioned on numerous occasions, we were informed she'd left the country to live with family in Europe. With the latest discovery, we've learned this is not the case. We haven't uncovered the whereabouts of Senator Madden's daughter as of yet, but as soon as more news breaks, we'll be here to keep you informed."

"Wow." My voice is filled with shock. I knew something would happen after getting my revenge on Kael's uncle. Yes, we made sure they found his body, but we also ensured that none of the evidence they found led back to us. Everything was done with exact precision.

"Are you okay, Phoenix?" His deep baritone sounds beside me, and I nod. I can't find words to describe how it feels to see your parents being arrested for being criminals. After all these years, growing up in that house, bred for a life of slavery. He knew what he was doing the whole time. Each year I got older, he planned for me to be taken into Caged. All for what? A seat in the senate. For fame. It makes me sick that my own father, the man who was meant to love and protect me, could do such a thing.

We never had any proof I was sold to Harlan, but now that the story is out and the media has a hold of it, my father will get what he deserves. The things he's done to earn a place on the senate will be made public knowledge.

Kael tugs me closer to him, cocooning me from the world, and I revel in it. "I love you, Kael."

"I love you too, baby. Always," he says into my hair. The scent of his spicy cologne calms me somewhat. This is the only thing I need. My new life is on the right track, and never again will I be in a situation where my choices are taken away from me.

Now all I want to do is move forward. Forget the past. It's my history, not my present or my future. With that in mind, I know I'll be with Kael, and even though the Wolfe name is smeared in filth, I know *my* Wolfe is a good man. And so is Samael.

I'm safe. I'm loved. I'm free.

Kael

TWO YEARS LATER

LIFE HAS BEEN MUCH SIMPLER NOW THAT THE PAST IS BEHIND us. Paige is finally free of the nightmares that plagued her for so long. There were nights I didn't know how we were going to make it through this.

She'd wake up screaming. I'd hear her begging, pleading for the pain to stop. It's then that I wanted to kill the monsters of her past all over again. I'd rage in the studio so she wouldn't know how much it was killing me to see her like that. After Harkin's murder, we'd slowly moved on. She went to see a therapist to talk through her anguish. We went to counseling together as well. I was there for her every step of the way.

I've seen the change in her. Over the last two years since her father was arrested along with her mother, she's become happier. The stress has left her, and now the only thing she worries about is the baby. Her pregnancy came at a time when we were both ready. And I couldn't be happier to see her glowing.

It's late afternoon and I've just finished the painting that's earned me a hefty commission. We decided to move closer to Sam and Freya in New York, but the house in Chicago still needs to be sold. Paige said we should keep it as a vacation home, but I want to move on.

Over the last three years, Samael and I have grown closer, perhaps like we used to be when we were kids and Mom was still around. Even though I don't remember much about her, I recognize the familiarity in Sam's eyes. The same deep blue.

"Uncle Kael!" A screech comes from down the hall, and not long after, my three-year-old niece comes bounding into the room. She's beautiful. I tell her she looks nothing like her father, but she always giggles and tells me her mommy says she's exactly like my brother.

Moment's later, Paige comes rushing into the studio gripping her swollen belly. "Layla!" she gasps, staring at the little blonde pigtailed girl in my arms. Paint is smattered across my clothes, which in turn has messed up the pink dress that Layla's wearing.

"Sit down, baby." I smirk at my woman. She's six-months pregnant with our first child, and I've never been more in awe of her. Even though she's been told to stop working so much, she can't stay away from the new dance studio she opened when we moved here. Freya and Kota now work alongside Paige, teaching dance to women of all ages.

Since we've moved closer, the girls have found companionship—a family of sorts, even though we're unconventional. Paige and Kota still enjoy playing together, mainly to taunt Axel and I. It's been good for them to have the connection, something their own families didn't give them.

"Freya is on her way to pick up the kids, but Mikael fell asleep so you'll have to carry him to the car when she gets here," she informs me. Mikael is a sweet kid. Looks just like his dad. Big blue eyes that will one-day break hearts.

"You ready to go home? Your mom and dad must be missing you," I murmur into her blonde pigtails. She smells of candy and soda. "Did she have the red candy in the jar?" I glance at Paige and she blushes with a slight nod.

"Those were the only sweets we had. I'll get more later."

"I had plans for those." With a wink, her cheeks redden, and I'm dying for some alone time with my wife. "Later." Setting

Layla down, I grab a cloth and wipe her dress, but the bright red and blue blobs on the front are not coming off.

"Mommy will yell at you," she informs me, and I nod. Freya is a feisty little thing. My brother has his hands full.

"Hello." The call comes from downstairs, and I hear her footfalls near as she heads up to the studio. Once inside, Freya glances between her daughter and me, and I can tell she's about to lose her shit.

"I picked her up not thinking." I shrug, and am met with intense green eyes, which remind me of my woman's.

"You're buying her a whole new outfit, Kael Wolfe," she sasses me playfully.

"Happily. I'd do anything for my little pixie." I press a kiss to her forehead, and she races over to her mother. "Where's Sam?"

"He's with Dax. They just signed the paperwork on a new club in Belize. We're thinking of heading out there for a couple of weeks. You guys should join us. It will be good to get away for a while."

"Sounds good, maybe we can make it a group getaway. I know Axe and Kota would want to get away as well." I glance at Paige, who's been quietly sitting in the corner of my studio at the laptop, her hand absentmindedly circling her belly.

"Paige?" Freya's tone is filled with concern, and it's only when I glance between them that I notice my girl's eyes glistening with unshed tears. Within an instant, I'm on my knees in front of her, my hands on hers.

"Are you in pain? What's wrong? Why are your crying?" The questions I bombard her with are non-stop, and she glances at me with a small smile. "What?"

"I just opened the email from Dr. Gysen. Look." She points at the screen as we all huddle over the desk. He just emailed a short video of our sonogram. In the email, he explained that he'd previously missed it but asked if we could come in for another one, because he's certain there are twins in my wife's belly.

"Baby," I murmur in awe. I couldn't love her more, at least I didn't think I could, but it seems every day this woman gives me more and more reason to be in complete and utter awe of her. Of the strength, love, and compassion she exudes. The life she's given me is beyond anything I could have ever asked for.

"Congratulations you two! I need to tell Sam."

I glance at my sister-in-law and I can't help nodding. I want him to be here. To be a part of my life. I've finally got the family I've always wanted, and to see my brother become a man unlike my father—a person who did the right thing instead of hurting people—makes me proud to call him brother.

"Yes, we're going to celebrate," I announce, planting a soft kiss on my wife's cheek.

BONUS SCENE

Paige

THE CHAIR IS COMFORTABLE, BUT MY ARMS PROTEST AT BEING bound above my head for so long. Kael stalks into the room with his chest bare and I can't help grinning. The man is a walking piece of art. "Something funny, Phoenix?" I shake my head quickly. His deep growl is evidence that he's in need of release.

We're playing a scene and with him it's different. As much as he thinks he's inflicting pain, he's never as bad as the man I had to endure for those long painful years.

Unzipping his paint-splattered jeans, he pulls out his thick cock. Without a word, he steps toward me and teases my mouth with the arousal coating my lips. I open, allowing him entrance. A groan, low and deep, rumbles from his chest. "Such a pretty bird." He slides in, then out, with such precision and restraint but I know he's barely holding on.

When his hips move faster the soft gagging sounds filter up to him and he watches me.

Our gazes lock—lust-fueled and desire driven.

This is fucking and most people think there isn't love

involved, but it overflows between us like a river raging toward the ocean.

This is us. Perfect. Complete.

Yes, when we're not in this room we're an average couple. But in here, I'm his pet, he's my Master and I wouldn't have it any other way. His hips buck and his cock hits the back of my throat repeatedly and my body aches for more, for him, for a good hard fuck.

"You want me, baby?" He slowly pulls out and leans in, his face inches from mine. Saliva drips from my chin, my lips are swollen, and I'm sure my eyes are glazed.

"Yes, Sir." My mouth quirks, and he grins like the salacious devil he is. The man who stole my heart and my soul. Yet, I gave it willingly.

Helping me onto the bed, he proceeds to tie my arms above my head with soft black rope.

"Open those pretty legs for me, pet." His fierce growl is enough to get my pussy wet. He only calls me that when we're playing, when I'm leashed and bound. My thighs spread easily, obeying my Master. If someone had told me that I would be owned by a man—the same man who had stolen my heart when I was eighteen—and be collared and leashed, I would have laughed in their face.

If someone had told me I was going to walk out of Inferno with my hand in his, I would have told them to cut the crap. And if someone had warned me I'd find love, well, I would have called the mental institute and had them admitted.

But here I am, bound to Kael's bed, the soft rope biting into my wrists, and the collar tightening just enough so that I have to focus on my breaths. It's part of the scene, focus, intensity, and desire. "Look at that wet cunt. Is it all for me, pet?" When he's in this mood his mouth is pure filth, and I love it.

"Yes, Sir." *Whack!* The soft leather of the flogger stings my thighs and I whimper. *Whack!* The bite this time is directly on my bundle of nerves, the throbbing of my clit sends me spiraling, but I know better than to let go and come.

I take deep breaths, slow and steady. "Are you hungry, Firebird?" The nickname he gave me filters through the haze of lust and I nod. *Whack!*

"Yes, Sir!" I cry out as another harsh bite on my clit has my body teetering on the edge.

"Good girl." The deep baritone of his voice drips lust. The cuffs around my wrists are unlocked and my arms fall beside me. My muscles ache from being in the same position for so long. "Lie back, I want your head over here." He points to the edge of the bed and I scamper to him. Positioning myself with my head at the right angle for his cock to drive into my throat, I wait.

Anticipation fuels my blood and my body hums with need. Thick, long, and hard, his cock is positioned perfectly. "Open." My mouth instinctively waters as I open it to accept my gift.

The beautiful erection that's only for me. Without warning he plunges into my mouth gagging me in the process and it takes me a minute to adjust. "Take it, pet. Every fucking inch, swallow my dick." And I do. Happily.

His hand finds my drenched sex and his agile fingers tease me, opening my smooth lips and I hear the growl. "So pretty and pink, dripping for me." He talks to no one in particular, but continues driving into my mouth. Then I feel it. The vibrator that torments me. It lightly touches my clit, teasing it with the soft hum.

He knows how to keep me edged to the point of pain. The physical ache to come, to feel my release shoot through my body, it's just out of reach.

Suddenly, he stops and pulls out of my mouth. "I need to be inside you." Hastily, I drop my feet to the floor and bend over the bed. The crown of his cock teases my pussy, and I wait for it, but it never comes because he plunges deep inside my ass. My cries are loud as I scream his name. The feel of him inside me is overwhelming, and the sting of his hand on my ass sends me into another fucking dimension. But I hear his order. "Come for me, pet. Now."

My body explodes. My head is reared back as he tugs on my long red hair. My back arches and his hips slam into my ass. The slapping sound of flesh echoes through our bedroom, and I tighten around him so much that I'm sure I won't be able to sit for a week.

"Such a perfect woman," he growls. I know he hasn't come yet, but he doesn't slow his assault on me, and my body isn't allowed to come down from the high because his cock is pulled from my ass. I hear the slick sound of him pulling the condom from his shaft before he pistons into my pussy, unraveling me a second time. He reaches around and tugs on the metal chain that's attached to the clamps on my nipples. The cry that's wretched from my body, along with the orgasm that's ripped from my core, have my eyes shutting so tight I see sparks, black, then white, then nothing.

My Master.

My Lover.

My Man.

THE WOLFE & HIS PHOENIX

Your fire burned my darkness,
My love healed your wounded soul.
Together we embark on our forever

You are my Firebird,
I love you, my Phoenix,

You are my Predator,
I love you, my Wolfe.

PLAYLIST

The Music

Rise - Katy Perry

Feels - Kiiara

Bunny Park - Cnsrd, Laco

Nights Like This - W. Darling

Ride - SoMo

The Kill - Thirty Second To Mars

River Full of Liquor - Leon Else

The Phoenix - Fall Out Boy

The After You - MiaKoda

D.D. - The Weeknd

You Are Here - Denmark + Winter

My Hell - Aaron Richards

The full playlist is available on Spotify

THE SERIES

Reading Order

The Forbidden Series will comprise of four full length novels, as well as two shorter novellas.

From the Ashes - A Forbidden Series Novella
Crave - Forbidden Series Book #1
Covet - Forbidden Series Book #2
Lust - Forbidden Series Book #3
Ache - Forbidden Series Book #4
Untitled Novella to come

These are standalone's and do not have cliffhangers.
Please note: They are dark romance reads with triggers.

THANK YOU

Acknowledgments

I can't believe the time has come to say goodbye and send Kael and Paige back into the book world. Their journey started last year, a short novella, nothing more. And when you all met them and fell in love with them as much as I did, I couldn't wait to tell you their full story. And what a journey it was.

This couple will hold a special place in my heart as my first dark romance ever. And when I stepped outside my comfort zone and delved into the darkness, you were there to catch me and encourage me to keep going. You asked for more and I can't thank you all enough.

Before I get all soppy, I must thank my husband for being my support on this journey. He makes sure I'm fully supplied with coffee which I then turn into roller coasters of emotion for you to devour. Love you, babe!

My Alpha BETAs!! You ladies are the SHIT! Becca, Kate, Lisa (Mrs. Kael Wolfe), Kenzie, Lizzie, Tamara, and Cat. Thank you for reading this story from it's first draft to the final proof.

My editor, Vanessa and proofreader Jessica, at PREMA for all their hard work, input, and advice in making this story so much more than it was. For taking my words and making them shine! I have no idea where I'd be without you ladies.

The Street Team, you ladies work your ass off to get my name out there, thank you! Tre, Tam, Becca, Renee, and the rest of the ladies, from the bottom of my little black heart, THANK YOU!

My Dreamers!! This group is like my own personal form of therapy. Thank you!! There is never a dull moment, and that's what makes me thankful for your love and support. It's not easy working with the intense stress and deadlines, but you always seem to brighten my day!

To my fellow authors who are there with advice, support, and just a general pick me up. Thank you. It means more to me than you know. Thank you for sharing my work with your readers, and giving me a friendship that is second to none.

A special thank you to Jane Anthony for being a friend like no other. A fellow author who listens to my rants, who offers support, advice, and just some good laughs. Thank you, lady you really are an incredible friend, and an amazing author!

To the bloggers, you ladies read, read, read, support, post, review, and you do it with a smile. Thank you!! We wouldn't be here if it weren't for you, so keep what you're doing, we appreciate you! #AllBlogsMatter!

Lastly, to the readers, thank YOU! It's because of you I'm able to put out book after book. Giving you what you ask for, and hopefully making you excited about the next book. Thank you for your reviews, keeping them SPOILER FREE ;) But most of all, thank you for buying our books. For your support, love, and encouragement.

THANK YOU!

D x

ABOUT THE
Author

Dani is a USA Today Bestselling Author of dark and deviant romance with a seductive edge.

Originally from Cape Town, South Africa, she now lives in the UK with her better half who does all the cooking while she writes all the words. When she's not writing, she can be found binge-watching the latest TV series, or working on graphic design either for herself, or other indie authors. She enjoys reading books about handsome villains and feisty heroines, mostly dark, always seductive, and sometimes depraved. She has a healthy addiction to tattoos, coffee, and ice cream.

www.danirene.com

info@danirene.com

OTHER BOOKS

by Dani

STAND ALONES

Choosing the Hart

Love Beyond Words

Cuffed

Fragile Innocence

Perfectly Flawed

Black Light: Obsessed

Among Ash and Ember

Within Me (Limited Time)

Cursed in Love (collaboration with Cora Kenborn)

Beautifully Brutal (Cavalieri Della Morte)

TABOO NOVELLAS

Sunshine and the Stalker (collaboration with K Webster)

His Temptation

Austin's Christmas Shortcake

Crime and Punishment (Newsletter Exclusive)

Malignus (Inferno World Novella)

Virulent (collaboration with Yolanda Olson)

Tempting Grayson

SINS OF SEVEN SERIES

Kneel (Book #1)

Obey (Book #2)

Indulge (Book #3)

Ruthless (Book #4)

Bound (Book #5)

Envy (Book #6)

Vice (Book #7)

THE TAKEN SERIES

Stolen

Severed

FOUR FATHERS SERIES

Kingston

FOUR SONS SERIES

Brock

CARINA PRESS NOVELLAS

Pierced Ink

Madd Ink

BROKEN SERIES

Broken by Desire

Shattered by Love

THE BACKSTAGE SERIES

Callum

Liam

Ryan

FORBIDDEN SERIES

From the Ashes - A Prequel

Crave (Book #1)

Covet (Book #2)

FIND ME

Online

Do you follow me?
If not, head over to any of the below links,
I love to hear from my readers!

Amazon

BookBub

Facebook

Facebook Group

Goodreads

Twitter

Pinterest

Instagram

Website & Store

Newsletter

Spotify

Made in United States
Orlando, FL
15 September 2022

22467344R00157